FRANK RONAN

Frank Ronan was born in 1963 in Ireland. His first novel, THE MEN WHO LOVED EVELYN COTTON, won the 1989 *Irish Times*/Aer Lingus Irish Literature Prize and his third novel, THE BETTER ANGEL, will be published by Sceptre in 1993. He lives in Normandy and Dublin.

Frank Ronan

A PICNIC IN EDEN

Copyright © 1991 by Frank Ronan

First published in Great Britain in 1991 by Bloomsbury Publishing Ltd

Sceptre edition 1992

Sceptre is an imprint of Hodder and Stoughton Paperbacks, a division of Hodder and Stoughton Ltd

Printed and bound in Great Britain for Hodder and Stoughton Paperbacks, a division of Hodder and Stoughton Ltd, Mill Road, Dunton Green, Sevenoaks, Kent TN13 2YA (Editorial Office: 47 Bedford Square, London WC1B 3DP) by Clays Ltd, St Ives plc.

British Library C.I.P.

A CIP catalogue record is available from the British Library

ISBN 0-340-56845-3

BOOK ONE

Nature ordains that we should begin with a sexual act. We are concerned with Dougie Millar, who had his beginnings in the attics of this house on the fourteenth of October 1956. His mother lay still with her hands in the small of her back, and his father breathed heavily as he gave the final push of his backside. Perhaps it is an imposition to tell you these facts so early in the narrative, but that is how it happened. The damp hairy flesh gave a final heave and shudder, and his father made an exclamation that would have been beneath the dignity of any animal, and lodged his seed inside her. Not deep, by most standards, but far enough to be the makings of a fat spoiled baby, in time to be the image of his father. The woman below him screwed up her eyes in disgust and tried to push him away as he collapsed on her in his petit-mort. He recovered and tried to kiss her neck, but she twisted away and said something sharp to him. He was too heavy with drink and satisfaction to argue with her and so he rolled away and slept, wiping his genitals with the sheets as he moved.

Annie Millar, the woman, had met this man at a dance in Achacloaigh on the same evening. It was her half-day off and she had walked to the dance by herself, about six miles by the good road. She was a plain strong girl from the Islands and she had an air of determination about her. She had some sort of idea in her head, or it may have been a premonition; in any case it was the sort of idea that can only be defined after its execution. Since running away from her family in Tiree at the age of seventeen she had spent her time working in a hotel in Oban and then came to domestic service here. The work wasn't bad, and she was well trained. At home, her mother would

3

have beaten her with a hairbrush if the gridiron wasn't blackened to her specifications. Annie was twenty-two on the night of the dance and she had recently heard of her father's death.

At the dance, she sat on the bench that ran along the side of the hall, with the plainest and the shyest of the girls, and watched the men come and go. Because she had been brought up in the Wee Free church she still had a sense of triumph in being at a dance at all. Perhaps it was because of this that there was nothing pathetic in her air of expectancy, unlike the girls on either side of her. She sat as though she was waiting for someone in particular, and when a man approached her from time to time to ask her to dance she would deflect him with a glare and light another cigarette.

In between the songs all the men would desert the hall, leaving the girls they had been dancing standing in the middle of the floor, and crowd outside to where they had their whisky stashed amongst the undergrowth. They lit and gasped at cigarettes and muttered and relieved themselves. When the music started again they would drift back in and begin to cast around for a partner. Often the incoming crop of men would differ slightly in its constituents as some remained outside with the drink and others rolled in from the pubs. About three-quarters through the evening, Iain MacLeod rolled in with the opening chords of an Elvis Presley song.

He was long and gaunt and hungry-looking. He had straight black hair and pale tight skin drawn over his bones at geometric angles. There was no mark or freckle on his skin and he had no lips to speak of. His eyes were full of misery, regardless of his mood. He was quite drunk, but still walking steadily. Annie Millar stood up and he came towards her. He said, 'Will you dance?' and she said, 'I will,' and they began to dance. It was done so naturally and with such style that nobody noticed except themselves. Anyone watching would have assumed that they already knew each other.

If dance had been all they did that evening, who knows? She might have been able to fall in love with him before she had to make love to him, and they might have produced some other child with a happier future. She used to say in later years that Iain MacLeod was the handsomest man she had seen. But by that stage she was saying it as a warning against handsome men. In any case, she carried things a little too far. She came to the dance with an idea and she went away with a man.

4

If you are plain, and you want someone who considers themselves handsome to go home with you, it is not as difficult as you might imagine. You can try simple flattery, as most people are well disposed towards flatterers. But you can be more subtle than that, and you can give someone the impression that you concur exactly with their self-image. This is complicated because the vainest people often despise themselves, and it is difficult to tell the true narcissists from those whose vanity disguises self-loathing. The simple and universal solution is to give someone the impression that they are hideous and despicable in reality, but that you are the only person who doesn't think so, or in extreme cases, the only person who is prepared to overlook it. In the case we are concerned with, Annie Millar was immoderately successful in allowing the young man she had just met to think that she understood him completely. Not by calculation, for she was not a woman who possessed that sort of intelligence; perhaps by intuition, or more likely by luck. She admired him and was careless of him at the same time, which was more or less the way he felt about himself at that stage of his youth, and so she swept him up in Achacloaigh, and with the music still pounding in their ears she carried him home with her.

With the sweat of the dance still on them and their heads thumping in the silence, she had to use all her strength to keep him from falling into the ditches on either side of the road between Achacloaigh and here. It was a warm evening for October and the road in those days was unpaved. She gripped him round the waist and pushed her head into his armpit like a crutch or a buttress, and got him here by determination. At intervals, with his free hand, he took the bottle of whisky from his jacket pocket and slugged at it. He stopped every half mile or so and howled like an animal. The whisky had given him a raging thirst, and so they had to stop at every burn and spring by the road so that he could lie down and thrust his face into it. There are seven burns and springs that you could drink from on that road now, but there may have been more before the forestry.

She must have wondered what she was doing as he stood and howled, with his legs braced and his face to the moon, but she was a woman to finish a thing once she had started it. When they came near Inverclachan, this place where I am sitting now, she warned him to be quiet and not to wake the Goodlands, who were the family in residence here, even then. There was something in the voice she used that made his obedience to her automatic, and eventually they fell through the back door and into the kitchen. At that time the kitchen was entirely her domain. She was the only servant employed here. She sat at the table and rested herself.

She thought about making tea for him, and then thought better of it, and gave him a tumbler of cooking-brandy instead. She knew that the best way of keeping a Highlander active is to keep the drink flowing through him. He sat across the kitchen table from her with a big dirty grin on his face, and from time to time he snorted like a horse. You or I might have been charmed by that and grinned back; we might have been drunk ourselves; but Annie Millar was working out how to get him to the attics without waking the household. The back stairs ran past the boys' rooms. She told him to take his shoes off and she lit a candle. Then she put her face to his and thrust her tongue between his teeth. She told him not to breathe. Once she had focused his attention in this way she led him towards her bedroom.

By now it had occurred to him that he was in love. There was no other reason he could see for allowing himself to be manipulated by such a plain and forceful girl. He had never felt like this for a girl before, not even in drink, and what he failed to understand he chose to call love.

He amazed himself with his performance. He thought that his groans were poetry and his hip-movement Presleyan. He thought he had never done a thing so well or enjoyed himself so much. The heat he generated in his own head led him from the suspicion to the conviction of love. By coincidence, she was thinking of Elvis also, or trying to, to take her mind off the goings-on above her. She was glad that she had kept her nightdress on and wished that her legs weren't bare. She was revolted by the softness and smoothness of his skin and kept her hands away from him as much as possible. Until then she had thought that the skin on a man's body must be as rough as the skin on her father's hands and face. She had never had sex with a naked man before. And even his thing seemed to her to be too soft and wormlike. She kept her eyes shut and regretted having brought him back. She had thought that good looks would be a guarantee of something, and she had thought that he would be cool and hard and alien. Instead she found herself being slobbered and sweated on.

Perhaps it was drink, or perhaps it was innocence, that misled Iain

MacLeod where the reactions of Annie Millar were concerned. But there are many people who assume that the act of love is symbiotic; that if two people become one flesh they must be feeling the same sensations. When he flung off his clothes and stood before her like one of those idiots painted by William Blake, he thought that she averted her eyes because of the blinding light that emanated from his flesh. When she pushed him away with a shudder he thought that he had worn her out with his passion and she could take no more. When he wiped himself on the sheet he thought that he was leaving her a gift to remember him by. He thought that while he slept she would be watching his face through the night, longing to touch it, but afraid of waking him.

In the morning, he was surprised to find himself where he was. She shook him awake while it was still early enough to be dark so as to get him away out of the house before the family were up. He sat up in bed, blinking in the electric light, and tried to remember what had happened the night before. The main thing that he was able to recall was that he had fallen in love, and so, like a gosling out of its shell, he looked around him for an object of his love and attached his affection to the first moving thing in his line of sight. At the foot of the bed there was a woman pulling thick stockings over square thighs. As she leaned forward her hair fell over her face, and when she was finished she put her arms up to pin it back. Her elbows were red and her underarm hair was thick. In spite of his headache he watched her with some curiosity, and wondered why sights which, by all the known laws of aesthetics, should have revolted him, engrossed him completely. Shivering with cold, he naturally enough mistook his morbid fascination and suffering for symptoms of love.

It is possible that this is the moment to concern ourselves briefly with a second conception. It will involve a sideways leap from Scotland to Co. Wexford and a forwards leap of several weeks. Unfortunately there is nothing interesting or dramatic in the conception of Adam Parnell. His parents were well married and he was the third of their five children. The night that brought him about was one of a series of acts in the dark; the edges of them blurred and run together so that they were as unmemorable as dreams. There was love in it, I suppose, perhaps. It was an act blessed by the Church and legislated for by the state and bound up in a contract. And love would not have been necessary to pluck Adam Parnell out of the air and insinuate him into a world where his christening mug and Pony Club tie were laid out and waiting for him.

It had been a long evening for Niamh Parnell after she had put the two children to bed. That charming man, her husband, Christian Parnell, was late home, as he was most nights. He usually said that he had met a man, and they had to talk business, and of course the only place you can talk is in a pub. Because they had only been married four years she always believed him. I think she may have been in love with her husband. Faith is one of the great drawbacks of love. It would never have occurred to her that his primary motive for spending the evening away from her was drink, because she had never seen him drunk. Indeed, at that stage of their lives, Christian Parnell himself was unaware that he had a problem with drink. He was still in his twenties, and on the verge of making his fortune, which was why he had to spend so much time talking to men in pubs.

What marked this night out from other nights, apart from Adam

Parnell's conception, was that it was Niamh's birthday and, while she usually tolerated her husband's lateness with a certain amount of good humour, being someone who was still in love, she was furious at the thought that he had forgotten the date. But when he arrived it was with a big flourish; with an armful of chrysanthemums and a string of pearls. He wished her a happy birthday and she was silent for a moment or two. She had been prepared to forgive him for forgetting. His memory was never the best. But he had remembered and turned up at midnight all the same. There was nothing she could say to him, because for the first time she had an inkling that he was not the person she had fallen in love with. In some ways she remained in the dilemma that had begun that night for the next seventeen years, and was released from it only by her death.

Her dilemma was something that is common enough among those of us who have the misfortune to be capable of falling in love, because we never fall in love with a reality. We fall in love before we have the chance to study the other person properly, and by the time we could know them well, we are so blinded by love that we cannot know them at all. And so love makes a misery of our lives as the daily evidence of the real person contradicts the person we believe them to be. Niamh Parnell, for a woman of her intelligence, had it badly. Even when things were at their worst, it never occurred to her that the boyish, gawky dreamer she had married should grow up a little. She always saw him the way she had seen him first; playing tennis with his arm in a sling, and laying side-bets on every point.

That first glimmer of discomfort was soon overcome by chrysanthemums and pearls and the man himself. He kissed her on the neck, because she disliked being kissed on the mouth, and he mumbled something that she didn't catch, but neither did she ask him to repeat it, because she wanted to think that he was telling her that he loved her; and then they went away to bed, to conceive Adam Parnell in their nightclothes with the lights off.

If you are one of those people who believe in reincarnation, and I am not, you will know about an attractive theory among certain Buddhists that there are four separate states of existence. The three most obvious are conception, life and death, but there is an interesting fourth which occurs between dying and reintroducing yourself to life. Supposedly you spend this time as a precocious six-year-old child with supercharged sensitivity, dashing around the atmosphere and seeing things you didn't ought to, until you finally catch sight of your next parents having it away in the act of making you. As your father reaches his climax, you experience a mind-blowing orgasm yourself, which makes you forget everything and begin a new life.

Although this may seem irrelevant, it occurs to me that it is a useful way to explain the recognition between people at their first meeting, when they are destined to become friends or lovers or enemies. It is possible chronologically that Dougie Millar first met Adam Parnell in this intermediate state, and not thirty-two years later. It would explain why, when they first saw each other as men, there was not only a certain amount of recognition, but a sort of disappointment in each other, as if they had known each other as airborne immortals, and were now faced with the sordid reality of a human on two legs, and how, despite this, they fell into a familiarity that is not easy to reason away.

It isn't that I believe any of this; but there is no accounting for what you might be led to believe. And my disbelief is no reason for you to dismiss a theory. For instance, I would never believe that an aeroplane could stay in the sky, but I found myself being hurtled about on them all the same. And if planes can fly, there is no reason to assume that invisible six-year-old brats cannot. And if we are going to go through with this, we might as well say that Dougie Millar and Adam Parnell collided somewhere over the coast of Manchuria between their existences, and had a month or two of shooting round the planet together until disaster struck on the west coast of Scotland the night of the fourteenth of October 1956, and young Dougie found himself shuffling his coil back on.

Which brings us back to the fifteenth of October and this house. The morning after the great act, Annie Millar smuggled Iain down the back staircase and made him a bacon sandwich and pushed him out the door to find his own way back to Achacloaigh in the gloom of the early morning. She could not bring herself to speak to him at all, but with the state his head was in he was grateful for the silence, and assumed that her taciturnity was as love-struck as his own.

As he went away down the back drive he got glimpses of this house between the trees. The back of this house is charming: there is something Italian about it. The front which faces the loch is severe and ugly and redeemed only by the view from it. Looking out of this window there is a flooded paddock below me and then the sea buckthorns and beyond them Loch Oban. On the far shore the hills begin. The furthest hills can be white this time of year, but it never snows here. We have the Gulf Stream and no more than a thick frost. It is a great place for camellias. They grow along the back drive, between the oak trees, in any place that hasn't been choked with rhododendrons. As the light grew stronger Iain MacLeod would have seen the flagpole at the top of the hill, above the birches, beyond which was the cottage that Adam Parnell was to come and live in. He would have walked past the door of Shore Cottage where his son, Dougie, was to live. If he had turned as he walked, he could still have seen the roof of the big house in the distance.

Throughout the next days and weeks he suffered from thoughts of Annie Millar in close conjunction with surges of lust. He was back at home in Alexandria with his mother, and working during the week. He had a small motor cycle which he rode the ninety miles out here to Inverclachan every Sunday. Annie allowed him to sit at her kitchen table for a quarter of an hour each time; gave him a cup of tea and sent him home again. He would spend most of the quarter-hour staring at the scrubbed deal below his elbows in embarrassed silence.

On the ride out, he could hold his nose into the wind in expectation, knowing that he had the power to knock her flat on her back with one look. He could bang on the side door of the house and stride into the kitchen without waiting for an answer, and stand square with his back to the range and know for two seconds that he was irresistible to her. If she had ever looked him in the eye in those first seconds he might have been successful; but she always kept her back to him, or stuck her head in a low cupboard as if she hadn't heard him coming in. By ignoring him she would force him to cough and shuffle and say hello to her, and by the time she turned to acknowledge him he would be standing in an altogether different, more apologetic position.

She would say, 'It's you,' in a flat voice, and only then would she look at him properly, and his whole composure would be awkward and lost and impotent: he seemed not handsome any more, but foolish-looking. She would give him tea in silence, with no offer of cake, although a cake might be sitting on the table before him; and he would drink his tea quickly because of the frostiness of her atmosphere; because of her hardness.

After leaving her, he would shake with rage on the mountain roads all the way to Alexandria. That night he would dream of her and wake in the dark, sweating and stiff. Six days followed, of imaginary conversations with her; phrases that would win her over the next Sunday.

His mother, a widow named Margaret MacLeod, suffered along with him in all of this. Watching her son in torment, she guessed that there might be a girl at the bottom of it. But he said nothing to her and so there was nothing she could do. Being religious, her only solution was to pray for him. He used to accompany her to Mass sometimes, before he began to spend his Sundays chasing out to the Highlands and coming home to her blue with cold and shaking with frustration.

He kept his Highland expeditions up until the New Year, but made no progress with Annie. She could have barred the door to him, or arranged not to be at Inverclachan on a Sunday, but that would have attached too much consequence to his visits. At first her indifference was genuine, but later his passion and persistence amused her and she despised him for it. She saw that she was giving him just enough hope to bring him back the following Sunday, and every Sunday that brought him back brought him lower in her estimation. She delighted in his weakness, and at the sight of a big handsome man quivering at her table. If she had had a conscience she might have dealt him a killing blow, but she preferred to watch him die by inches. It was perhaps to punish him for the indignity she felt that she had suffered beneath him in her bed. Perhaps she hadn't much else to amuse her on a Sunday.

He bought her pearls for Christmas. A coincidence, perhaps, that he bought them at about the same time that Christian Parnell bought pearls for Niamh's birthday. Iain wrapped his present in blue paper and brought it to Annie's kitchen table. She was icing a cake and the air was sticky with fine sugar. He couldn't find a gap in the atmosphere to mention the package. At the end of his quarter-hour he drew it from his pocket and left it by the empty teacup. She didn't open the package until years later when she heard of his death. Once she had opened it she kept the pearls for a week, wondering what to do with them, and then she gave them to a friend of hers, who was going to Glasgow, to sell them for her.

His New Year resolution for 1957 was never to see her again; not think of her if he could help it. It was a serious resolution; well made and with every possibility of succeeding. He was still at an age when he could recognise the moment to save himself. He began to spend his Sundays in Alexandria again, not perhaps going to Mass with his mother, but drinking with men and talking to girls. A sort of equilibrium was restored to him and he put on a little weight. But his resolution could have taken no account of the existence of Dougie Millar.

As that sort of news will, the news of Annie's pregnancy leaked back to him. He had friends in Achacloaigh, and a thickening waist on a single woman is not a thing that goes unremarked in places like that. It was told to him in a hearty, manly way, as if he had had a lucky escape by dropping her in time, but after he heard it he became lost altogether. He saw Annie in a new light; and began to interpret her attitude as reticence; as nobility of spirit and selflessness. His vanity allowed him to believe that he was the sort of promising young man whose life a plain girl would be unwilling to burden and spoil. It would have been beyond him to understand that for Annie Millar his skin had the texture of a mollusc. Until he met her he had spent his life being treated as Apollo incarnate.

We can take a moment to bleed for Iain MacLeod. He was a man who believed that women were intrinsically good, as though they were a species or a breed apart. In retrospect, an attitude like this could be interpreted as sexist condescension. These days we are more inclined to judge people by their individual merits. But if Iain MacLeod was brought up by women to believe that cats were sly and sheep were stupid and women were sainted, then his attitude may not have been entirely his own fault. His mother and sisters, the only women he knew well, had loved him all his life, had polished his shoes and given him the truth in small doses. His mother was a woman whose motivations were always impeccable. A good person like this can have done nothing to prepare her son for the likes of Annie Millar.

When he heard the news of Annie's condition, the twist that had been lying in his gut for weeks past leapt up and seized him in the throat. You would think perhaps that the jolts shooting through him as he banged his motor cycle at full tilt along the unmade road from Inverary would have brought him to his senses; or the freezing air of the mountains on his ungloved hands, stuck tight to the handlebars with the cold. A man in his right mind would have wondered what he was rushing out here for; would have suspected that Annie Millar might smash his innocence and leave him emotionally mutilated for the rest of his life.

He found her in the garden and they walked to the shore. I don't know if I can bear to describe that scene to you. Has the knowledge that you are a fool ever come upon you forcefully and unexpectedly? Have you ever been caught doing that which no sane person would be seen at? Or realised that you were the only person in history to have believed all the myths and fallen in love: that for other people love is a thing to be manipulated and abused? By falling in love, I mean only that you value another person beyond your estimation of yourself, and put yourself in a vulnerable position as a result. It is a fact that you cannot be sure that anyone else has ever felt the same way about you. It is a fact that you have never met anyone whom you knew for certain had a conscience, or who cared for anything outside of themselves. Or, if you are someone who clings to a ridiculous faith in the people you love, and if all of this won't touch you, or can't mean anything to you, try to remember the one moment in your life when you were conned by the biggest of jokes, and you tried to be a good person and secure your place in heaven, and then you found yourself exposed, and people were laughing at you, and at the same time not believing your intentions. Never mind about Iain MacLeod and emotionally mutilated; try you and me and plain misunderstood.

Or never mind all that either. Sitting here, and by leaning a little to the left, I can see the place on the shore where she smashed his mind up. She was fat with child by the sea buckthorns, standing with her legs apart like a powerful woman, and she also had that air of ruthlessness that pregnant women can have: survival tactics. Iain stooped over her, all crumpled limbs, and a purple hand picking at the knee of his trousers; looking at the loch as though he would rather be drowned.

We are getting ahead of ourselves. The thought of killing himself hadn't yet crossed his conscious mind. But it is equally possible that Annie Millar was a woman with some sort of instinctive foresight. She may have sensed that streak of self-destruction in him that destroyed him in the end. She could have done worse in those days than marry Iain MacLeod. The thinking at the time was that a woman in her position could not afford to pick and choose. He was healthy and good-looking and he had a job. What more could she have asked for? When she did eventually marry, years later, she married a man who made Iain look like something that had been sent by God to her. But for some reason, the man who had impregnated her made her heave with revulsion, and she felt that by rejecting him she was preserving herself.

She said bitter things to him on the shore. She looked past him as she spoke, watching the head of a grey seal as it appeared and disappeared in the loch. His eyes, miserable at the best of times, darkened to indigo with tears.

'You are nothing,' she said. 'I'd kill myself before I'd marry you. No I wouldn't. Not if I could kill you first. Don't bother with your crying. If that is how you feel, go home to your mother. Do you know what you are? The sight of you makes me sick. I could vomit black bile.'

She walked away from under his shadow. The winter sun caught the side of her face as she came back this way. She spoke again as she walked, without turning or looking back.

'You have nothing to give me.'

By now the pupils of his eyes were a black colour. It is not a trait I have observed in anyone else, except this man and his son Dougie: the colour of their eyes would lighten to pale-blue with happiness and blacken with misery. It was an observation that served me well in later years with Dougie, who otherwise was so taciturn in his expression that most people assumed him to be miserable the entire time.

On the ride home Iain crashed his motor cycle. It was nothing very serious because he landed in some snow and only broke a few fingers. They were so cold at the time that he didn't know they were broken until he got back to Alexandria and his mother asked him why he was holding his hand so strangely. The fingers mended before the child was born.

The child was born in hospital in Oban. Although he was a large child, weighing nine and a half pounds, the midwife congratulated Annie on a short and trouble-free labour. Annie picked up a glass from her bedside locker and studied the veins that had broken in her face from straining and said, 'You try it.' When the registrar came to ask her what name she would give the baby, she said that she hadn't thought about it. The registrar said that Duguld was a good name. It had come into his head because that was the name that the woman in the next bed had given to her child. Annie shrugged her shoulders and said that it would do, and he wrote it down. It was Mrs Goodlands at the big house here who later began the practice of calling the boy Dougie.

Mrs MacLeod persuaded Iain to travel to Oban by train and see the two of them. It was a hard decision for her, but it was her nature to think the best of people and she was willing to allow that women often behaved strangely while they were pregnant, and that birth might have brought Annie to her senses.

He came and stood by her bed and she treated his arrival with her usual indifference. He knew the truth of things as soon as he saw her face, and would have liked to leave again without saying a word, but he wanted to see the child too, and so he spoke to her. She gave him that look that made all his handsomeness and cleverness desert him, and made him feel that he was not the sort of man who could conceive a child. And as there was no child to be seen by her bed, he began to wonder if there had been a child at all. Annie made no reference to Dougie; only answered Iain in monosyllables while studying a knitting pattern in a magazine. He twisted his head to read the magazine with her, thinking the pattern must be for wee booties or mittens for the baby; but instead it seemed to be for a feminine garment called a *fascinator*, to be edged in sequins and worn on the head by the intelligent party-goer, who knew only too well what a cold night could do to her looks and enjoyment.

There was something about the ludicrousness of the prose he was reading that restored some of his confidence, and he asked her at last where the child was. She fixed a stare on him as though what he had asked was mad or obscene. He would have lost courage if she had looked away, but she kept staring at him until he was forced to ask again. This time he rephrased it and asked if he could see his son.

'No,' she said.

Embarrassment overcame him. His face reddened and he looked about him to see how many of the other women in the ward had heard the exchange. They all had a studied air of preoccupation, but he could feel their hostility. They were gathered up on her side, assuming that he was the dishonourable sinner and that Annie was sinned against. They seemed as if they were prepared to defend her if he made trouble. He asked her quietly if he should come back at a better time.

She said, 'Don't bother yourself,' and turned the page of the magazine to a suggestion for an economical but stylish candlelit dinner.

He said goodbye to her and he went away. He passed a room with babies in it and stood in the door wondering which was his. They all looked more or less the same to him. He was disappointed that out of five babies he couldn't know his own by instinct. A nurse came

17

up behind him and asked if there was anything he wanted. He asked her which child was Annie Millar's. She pointed to one of the cots, but became suspicious when he asked her what the child was called.

'Are you a relation?' she said.

He said, 'I'm the father.'

She looked at him as if he was mad, and then she hustled him out of the room. She asked him if he would like to see Miss Millar, but he said no, that was all right, and left her.

He did manage to see the child a few more times over the next three years. He would borrow a car and drive down to Inverclachan whenever he had the courage. Once, when the child was two and a half, Annie allowed him to take Dougie to Achacloaigh for the afternoon. He met some of his friends and they went to the café and sat Dougie on the table and fed him ice-creams. He was tempted to kidnap the boy and bring him back to his mother to rear, but his friends talked him out of it, and Dougie was driven back here to Annie. It was just as well, perhaps, because kidnapping was not an act that his mother would have approved of or been willing to involve herself in.

Mrs MacLeod went to see Annie and Dougie once. It was not a successful meeting, with Mrs MacLeod thinking that her son had had a lucky escape by not marrying Annie, and Annie knowing it and being defensive. Mrs MacLeod asked her about her own family, and Annie lied and said that she was an orphan with no brothers or sisters, and then Mrs MacLeod began to pity her almost as much as she pitied Dougie; and Annie felt that she was being patronised, and went on lying about herself. She lied because she felt that those things were no one's business but her own, and because she was afraid that if Mrs MacLeod ever met her own mother the two of them would gang up on her.

I am beginning to understand Annie Millar. A lot of the time she was only afraid. Fear made her nasty, and nastiness gave her courage. I regret this insight into her character, because my concern is with Dougie Millar, and in his life she was the arch-villainess. If we are going to find reasons for forgiving Annie, how are we going to hate her for Dougie's sake? It does us little tangible good to see that behind the venom there was a child who was abused by Presbyterianism and her mother's hairbrush, and a person who had fear instilled in her from an early age and never had the intelligence to fight it on human terms.

Throughout the first years of Dougie Millar's life, his father continued to live in a small house above a tobacconist's in Alexandria with his mother and two of his sisters. The women of his household adored him, so that he not only had one of the two bedrooms to himself, but he had the larger one. The three women packed themselves into a room at the back. At least two of them would be out of bed an hour before him in the mornings, to warm the house and lay his breakfast and give his shirt a last run of the iron. Five, and sometimes six days a week he worked as a mechanic, maintaining the cranes in Clydebank. He was fond of his job, and considered it worth the long daily journey by motor cycle. He empathised with the cranes, because they were isolated from their surroundings by tallness, and you could imagine a vanity in them; a sort of arrogance. It was something he spoke about when he was drunk. He was the kind of young man who wore the collar of his boiler suit standing up, because he thought that it enhanced his looks. Something harmless enough in a boy of twenty.

After Annie Millar, the Alexandrian women set about patching his ravaged sensibilities. They packed him with comfort and adulation, and by pieces restored his ego to a semblance of its former magnitude. It took two years before he began to find their consideration oppressive, and looked about himself for other women. He grew tired also of working on the cranes and thought about enlisting. He saw himself in a Highland uniform, with a kilt to swing behind him and a feather in his cap.

He met Laura Baxter and fell in love again. By that I mean that he thought about her a lot, and went off his food, and had bouts of unexplained happiness. She was a normal girl whose ambition was normality. She was pretty in a washed-out way with thin blonde hair and small teeth. She was pleased to have his attentions because her friends seemed to envy her for having them. In her opinion he had been foolish to throw away his good job on the cranes to be a Guardsman, but she too liked the uniform, and she was thrilled by the idea that he might be asked to guard royalty.

He thought that this time he had got the thing right, and allowed himself to fall for Laura with all his old weakness. There was nothing strange or incomprehensible about her. She only wanted respectability, and expected no more of him than that he should behave exactly as other men did.

There was one aspect of his love for Laura Baxter that worried him. Although he had no doubt that he was in love, and she was seldom out of his thoughts, he had no physical passion for her. He wanted to feel lust for her, and he tried to feel it, but no matter how passionately he kissed her with his mouth the rest of him remained limp and uninterested. Being a good girl, she was unaware of this phenomenon. She saw it as a point in his favour that he never tried to take things too far. She was saving herself for her wedding night, and assumed that he was saving himself as well. But he was losing sleep over it; he tried to think of her while masturbating, and failed, while Annie Millar still only had to cross his mind for a moment for him to be creased with lust. He hoped that it would be sorted out after the marriage, but it occurred to him that to be able to make love to Laura he would have to think of Annie at the same time.

Neither did he ever manage to tell Laura about Dougie. He thought about it once or twice, but they never seemed to have the sort of conversation in which a matter like that could be brought up.

Soon after he had finished his basic training, and while he was home on leave, cutting a dash on the streets of Alexandria in his new uniform, he had his first epileptic fit. He was sitting at tea with his mother and his sister Mary on a Tuesday, when he stopped eating, with a forkful of food half-way to his mouth, and a fixed, distant expression on his face. His mother stared at the piece of square sausage on his fork, and asked him what the matter was, and when she got no answer followed his gaze out of the window. She was searching the street below to see what could be upsetting him, when Mary said, 'Look, Mam. Look at him.'

There was hysteria in her voice. Mrs MacLeod looked at her son. The fork in his hand was twitching like a diviner's rod, and the sausagemeat was plastered across the front of his uniform. An unearthly scream came out of him and he fell from his chair as stiff as a skittle. He lay on the floor for a few moments with his eyes bulging and the colour of his face darkening before the convulsions started.

He was seven minutes thrashing on the floor, like a mackerel in the bottom of a boat, knocking chairs over, while the women shrieked and cried, trying to hold him still so that he wouldn't hurt himself.

Afterwards, he swore them to secrecy about it. He must have hoped that it would never happen again, but it was only a matter of time before he had a fit in the barracks and the Army gave him an honourable discharge. The shame of being sacked from the Army was, if anything, even greater than the shame of being labelled an epileptic. He had invested a lot in his image of himself in uniform. But he still had Laura, and although she had gone quiet on the subject of marriage, that was not a thing he was in a condition to notice.

Within weeks of his discharge Laura found out about Annie, through a cousin of hers who had married a fisherman out of Achacloaigh. As a coincidence it was unlucky and badly timed, and perhaps her reaction was justified in that it was something that she should have been told about, and there was no evidence that Iain had any intention of telling her. Whether she was really that affronted by the scandal of it, or whether she was looking for an honourable escape, the effect was the same. She dropped him. There was no flaming row or long discussion, but she was the second woman to tell him what she thought of him in a cold voice, and send him home to his mother.

The shock of her rejection of him was delayed, partly because he was numbed already, and partly because he thought that she loved him and would return to him. There was still a shred of vanity in him that made him think he was irresistible, and he thought of Laura as a girl who would recognise this. She was, after all, the polar opposite of Annie Millar.

Twelve days after she broke with him, on a hot Bank Holiday, he was at Queen Street station in Glasgow with a friend of his, when he saw her stepping off a train in the company of a uniformed soldier. The soldier was a short young man with a smug, proprietorial air about him and a swagger in his walk. She was hanging on to his waist like a thing owned. Iain MacLeod went home and hanged himself.

The Alexandrian women were out of the house, away at devotions or something. He decided on hanging because he had heard that it involved an orgasm at the point of death. The irony of dying for Laura with an erection appealed to him. A private joke for himself alone.

He locked the door out of consideration for his mother, so that she would have to get a man to break it down, and it would be this man who found him swinging, and his mother would be told to stay out of the room and be spared the sight of him. He got out a pencil and a piece of paper to write a suicide note, but there was nothing he could think of to say and the paper was left blank. He sorted out certain of his possessions: his watch, small silver things, his scian dubh; and put them in an envelope which he marked with Dougie's name.

He spent perhaps five minutes standing before a mirror, as if he was committing his face to memory. He had spent a great deal of his life before the same mirror, and in the past the face that had looked back had been his greatest comfort. Catching his own eye in a mirror as he passed it had always made him smile, as though he were catching the eye of a lover; sometimes he would laugh outright. Now the face that he examined was immobile and strange to him. For the first time he saw the misery in his eyes that had always been apparent to everyone else. He could see no beauty, only a gaunt lipless man. He lathered his shaving brush and spread the soap over the mirror until he had blotted out the reflection, and then he began to remove the pegs from the clothesline he had brought up from the yard.

To get the height he needed, he had to open the hatch into the attic and tie the line to one of the rafters. He had also worked out that there was nothing but the rafters which would take his weight. He had thought that he would jump from a chair, but once he was in the attic it seemed more sensible simply to jump out of the hatch. He had taken his shoes off before going up into the attic, automatically, and while he was fitting the line around his neck he looked down at them on the floor. They were standing tidily side by side. He had had no intention of dying in his stockinged feet, and he wondered about going down again to put his shoes back on; but at the same time he realised that he couldn't risk something which might be a delaying tactic; he was afraid of changing his mind. He pulled at the rope twice to test it, and then, aiming himself at the toe-caps of his shoes, polished to military standards, he jumped.

The joke on Laura misfired. There was no erection or orgasm. Neither did his neck break, and so his death was slower than it might have been. Apart from the discomfort of the hanging itself, his last sensation in this world before he lost consciousness was the evacuation of his bladder.

The thing that Adam Parnell remembered most urgently about his childhood was diving below the level of the windows with his brothers and sisters; hiding behind the curtains as his mother bolted the doors of the house; and remaining hidden and silent until the danger was past. One of them would have heard a car approaching down the overgrown avenue; not that it could be called an avenue any more, since the alders had all been cut down for firewood: it was only a rutted lane, with stumps and honeysuckle and self-sown sweet peas gone wild. They would stay out of sight until the car had been identified, and in most cases they would wait until it had gone away again. The occupants of the car would bang on the doors and walk around the house and sometimes leave a note pushed through the letter-box. Occasionally, the car would turn out to be their father, and they would come out of hiding, thinking that it was only he, and not the enemy.

One of the burdens of childhood is that you are forced to take sides, and it wasn't until long after they had all left home that the Parnell children knew that the real enemy was their father. He had led them to believe that the entire world was bad, save Christian Parnell, and that he was an ill-used victim, the last honest man left on earth. This belief seemed also to be central to the faith that their mother had in her husband, and the idea was stretched by him so that even the children were made to feel that they were part of an unfair burden that the world had put upon him. Although it was not a thing that Christian Parnell was conscious of, he expected his children to resent themselves along with the rest of the world. They were taught to distrust themselves. It is terrible not to be allowed to trust yourself, and to be induced to love and trust someone who is out to destroy you.

In the thirteen years since Adam Parnell had been conceived, his family had moved house four times, and not in the cause of upward mobility, although the first move, it is true, was to grander circumstances than those into which he had been born. Confident that he was about to become a wealthy man, Christian Parnell sold the modest house that his parents had given him as a wedding present, and bought a rambling country house at the other end of the county, heavily mortgaged and in need of repair. The children were given ponies and Niamh Parnell set about colonising the rooms one by one. After her death, Christian was unkind enough to say that she ruined him with the amount of money she spent on that house, but he did nothing to prevent her at the time, and gave her every indication that he could afford whatever she wanted. To begin with, they lived a sort of idyll, which Christian celebrated daily in any public house he came across, while he continued to make plans for spending all the money he was about to make.

Most of the time you would have been hard put to detect signs of drink on him. He was not a man who fell over, nor was he ever violent. He was usually never at home in the day: he returned there to sleep, and breakfast was the only meal he ever ate in the house. And breakfast was not his best time of day. Between the hours of seven-thirty and nine he roared like a bull, so that his wife and children developed the habit, whenever it was possible, of staying in bed until he had left the house.

Of course, within a year it became obvious that their lifestyle in that house was insupportable. It took a further six months for Christian to work up the courage to confess the situation to his wife, and another six months for them to decide to sell the place, and a year after that before they found a buyer. The solution they hit upon was to sell everything except a disused farmhouse, which was in a deserted place called Williamstown on the western end of the property where the hills began. Just as she had made the house inhabitable, Niamh had to start again with a damp, rat-infested farmhouse in the rainshadow of a grey hill.

It was during those three years, between the ages of six and nine, before the move to Williamstown, that Adam Parnell developed the habit of gardening. His Aunt Bridget gave him packets of seed, to which he paid a phenomenal amount of attention, for a boy of his size, and she explained to him the layout of the old gardens as they must have been during the heyday of the house. Aunt Bridget was a woman who was blind to anything but plants, and she taught him all the Latin names, and the processes of propagation. Her own house and garden were only three miles away, and when she came over to see him, for he was the only member of his family that she had any time for, he would follow a pace behind her as she hobbled around the old garden, muttering in Latin and throwing cigarette ends beneath the shrubs.

Niamh was pregnant with her last child when they moved to Williamstown, and Nelly was only a year old. There had been several miscarriages between Adam and Nelly, and Niamh had been warned not to have any more children, but because she was so isolated, and saw so little of her husband, her children were her companions and she decided to have as many as possible. It could be said of this woman that her children were her great passion, and she felt lost without a baby around the place.

Still, they were not ideal circumstances for a house removal, and the place seemed dingy and cramped after the light and air of the other house, and there was a loss of freedom, because there had been sixteen bedrooms before, and Adam was in the habit of sleeping in a different room each night, because each room was haunted by a different ghost, and he enjoyed the company of each of them since they were all benign. The ghost he loved best – in fact he was in love with her – was a girl who haunted the smallest bedroom at the top of the house, and would come to kneel by his bed to say her prayers after he turned the light out. In the morning he would see her footprints on the damp of the linoleum where she had walked away from his bed. He would have seen that ghost every night if he could, but she would only appear to him after he had slept in all the other bedrooms first.

The other problem with Williamstown was that the house was too small to accommodate servants and too remote for girls to come in by the day. So a caravan was bought, and parked in the haggard, so that the two girls they retained could sleep in it, and privately Adam thought that the caravan made the place look even dingier, and they were becoming daily more like tinkers.

They lasted two years in their first period at Williamstown, before it had to be sold, and Christian Parnell rented a house for his family in the town, saying that it was all for the better and it would be so convenient for schools and shops. By the time they left Williamstown the caravan was empty because the two girls had left to get married, and Niamh said that it was easier to do the housework herself than to chase idle girls around all day. The roof blew off the caravan in a storm and nobody ever found it.

Williamstown was bought by the same people who had bought the big house, not for the house itself, but for the bit of land and the rights of way that went with it. The Parnells spent six winter months in the town, which Adam remembered as the worst six months of his childhood.

The day they moved into the town was the day that Christian Parnell first put himself into a clinic for drying out alcoholics. His family managed. Aunt Bridget paid the rent. Other relations sent regular boxes of food and clothing, and Niamh faced up to all the creditors and made arrangements where she could for them to be paid in weekly instalments, while at the same time she personally pursued any debtors and extracted what was due, so that by the time her husband was released things were almost on an even keel. They were bolstered, during these trials, by the caring and witty letters that Christian wrote them from the clinic. He painted a picture of a glorious future for them all once he was cured and reunited with them. He even used terms of endearment that included the word love, which was a shock to his children, and as strange to them as if he had used the word fuck in a letter. But they took it as an indication of the new man who had emerged in the course of his treatment, and it helped to convince them that life would be better once he was back. Similarly, they were encouraged by his accounts of his new passion for jogging, up to eight miles a day around the suburbs of Dublin, since the man had never been known to take physical exercise in his life before. They were not to know that the pub nearest the clinic was filled every morning by people in running shoes.

You may be wondering by now what exactly it was that Christian Parnell did for a living. That was a problem which his children also had to contend with. One day, while they lived in the town, Adam was given a form at school, which asked, among other questions, what his father's profession was. After school he sought out Thomas and James, his two older brothers, to compare notes on how they had answered it. Adam felt that he had come out best by answering that his father was a businessman. James had answered that he didn't know, and Thomas had said that Christian Parnell was a farmer, which was a lie, but had some basis in their recent ownership of the few acres of bog at Williamstown.

The fact was that Christian never really did anything for a living. He had been to university in Dublin for a term, but homesickness had driven him home, and so he was trained for nothing. During his twenties, his family had set him up in various small businesses, all of which had failed because his only business interest was in becoming an overnight millionaire, and because his only real interest was in drink. He had an aptitude for wheeling and dealing, which he practised in pubs, and which brought him lump sums of money on a sporadic basis. And he had the sort of charm that made people who didn't know him very well long to lend him money. He was very plausible.

After his release from the clinic he managed to keep his drinking secret for a month, and his family went around in a state of elated optimism, and Niamh believed that it wouldn't be long before they could move back out to the country, because she hated the town so much that every day in it was torture to her, and she saw her time there as a prison sentence. Her optimism was not wholly illogical. During the time when her husband had been away, when she had been in charge of things, it had become apparent to her that their situation was not insoluble, and once Christian was sober again they could easily become comfortable.

Adam was the first to know that his father was drinking again. He heard it from a boy at school whose mother had had a puncture outside a small country pub and gone in to ask for help. Christian Parnell had been the only customer sitting at the bar, and he had come out and changed her wheel for her, charm personified as usual, and even tried to buy her a drink, but she said no, she was in a hurry, and thanked him. He didn't know who she was, but she recognised him, because her son was the confidant of his son, and she had been following the family drama at a remove. While Adam was being told, he had a physical sensation that he was sinking into the ground, and it was the first time in his life that he had a suicidal impulse. He was eleven. The future closed down in front of him like a black wall, and he could see no hope for anyone. He decided that

27

as long as he lived he would never again believe what anyone said. He never spoke to that boy again, and cut him dead the next few times he met him, making an enemy of him.

The following ten days or so were difficult at home, because, faced with the faith everyone else seemed to have in his father, Adam felt that he had to keep his information to himself. When he could stand it no more and told his mother, she said that she already knew, and then she began to cry, and while he would normally have been able to put his arms around her and comfort her, this time he stood with his hands by his side, embarrassed and helpless. Both he and his mother knew that they had betrayed each other for the past few days by keeping the thing to themselves, and at that moment that seemed to be a worse betrayal than the one perpetrated by his father, because as a result of it they were isolated from each other, and as long as they were divided Christian Parnell could rule them.

The one thing that Niamh stuck out for, while she still had the energy, was that she would not remain in the town. If she was going to be poor and married to an alcoholic, she would rather do it in the privacy of the country, where she might have some dignity left to her. And Adam was persuasive in this too. He thought that he would die if he remained in the town, away from plants. They discovered that Williamstown had been unoccupied since they had left it in the autumn, and Adam went with his mother, without telling Christian Parnell, to see if they could rent it from the new owners.

Williamstown was not improved by being left empty for the six months of the winter. There were black freckles of damp in all the corners, and the rats had reinvaded the house and chewed the wiring. Niamh was puzzled by the sound of running water in the sitting-room, until someone lifted a floorboard to discover that a spring had broken ground beneath the floor and the whole house was sitting on water. But Adam had his garden again. He became a secretive child, who spoke to no one but his mother, and who usually found a reason for not attending school.

They carried on in a state of alternating crisis and hiatus, and what the children came to accept as normal life wore Niamh Parnell down until she succumbed to the illness that killed her. The symptoms of Christian's drinking remained at one remove from him: in the disappearing furniture that his wife sold to buy food, in the nervousness of his children. Years later, Adam told his sister Nell that he had lain awake at nights praying to God that his father would be killed on the roads and not return to them. Nell said that she had done the same thing, and when they spoke to the rest of the family about it they discovered that they had not been alone. He must have been a powerful man to have survived the death-wishes of all his five children, and return home, night after night, to disrupt the household.

Not that he would disrupt the household in any obvious way; but he brought his unhappiness back with him, and transferred that which he should have been feeling about himself on to those around him, and made them feel worthless.

I don't know why he drank. And I don't know whether he drank because he was such an inadequate human, or whether his inadequacy was due to his drinking. By the time we are talking about, it was a question that hardly mattered any more. When your personality has been submerged that deeply for that many years there is nothing to be saved from it. There must have been a man worth knowing at some point, because Niamh Parnell fell in love with him and married him, and the evidence suggests that she loved him until the day she died. In general she was an incisive woman who wouldn't suffer fools, and chose her friends with such circumspection that by the age of thirty she didn't have any; but still she managed to believe most of the things her husband told her. Perhaps his plausibility was her downfall. Perhaps we have to blame love, and the lesson of this is that one mustn't be fooled into falling in love. No good can come of it.

By not being the oldest of the Parnell children, Adam and James were saved some of the pressure that fell on Thomas. It was Thomas who bore the brunt of his father's argumentativeness (an argumentativeness which Christian demonstrated only in the presence of his children; among others he was a rational, sensible man). If Thomas aired an opinion on any matter, or even stated a fact, his father would flatly contradict him, without any regard for evidence or feeling. Adam listened in amazement once, as his father set about proving to Thomas that the Boer War had taken place in northern Africa, and Thomas trembled and stuttered with rage, pointing helplessly at the pages of history books, to which his father would respond, without deigning to look at the words, 'Books! What are you going to find out from books? If books are where you get your information, you won't get to know much about life. I am your father. I know more than you do. I don't need a book to tell me where the Boer War was fought.' At the time Adam thought his father unspeakably stupid. It wasn't until twenty years later that he realised that the Boer War had nothing to do with it. That the object of the exercise was to antagonise and humiliate Thomas, and thereby Christian Parnell could consolidate his domination of his children.

Thomas left home for the first time when he was thirteen years old, and spent six weeks on a herring trawler. He managed to contract a mild dose of tuberculosis while at sea and was forced to come home again, but he was always itching to be away. Williamstown was too isolated for him, under the hill with no neighbours within a half mile of the place. After his scorching rows with his father he would march out of the house, towards the town, not reappearing for days, and then only to ask for money. People thought that he was a child with problems, and it was great surprise to everyone that he became so wealthy at such an early age.

James was quiet, and apparently well balanced. When he did speak up it was to take his father's side in an argument, or to make excuses for him when he wasn't there. James was always trying to be the peacemaker. It seemed, in his adolescence, that there was a lot of goodness in James, which was easily forgotten years later when he acquired the ruthlessness that is necessary for dealing in heroin.

And then, before the girls, there was Adam. Adam found himself watching Thomas closely so that he could know how to avoid trouble for himself. So everything that Thomas did, Adam was inclined to do the opposite. Thomas's vulnerability to conflict taught Adam to make himself invisible before his father. Adam became one of those children who keep to their rooms, unless he was out in the garden. His only aim in life seemed to be to be left alone with his plants in silence. The world could be falling in around their ears, and he would be out with his Aunt Bridget, drooling over some pink thing growing in a ditch. It was not an interest that his parents perceived as a practical way of making a living. His father would find him picking over a seedbox on his bedroom windowsill, when he should have been doing homework, and shout at him, accusing him of amusing himself. It was a memory that was unpleasant to him until he won his first gold medal at the Chelsea Flower Show, and after that it amused him to think of it.

He spent all the time he could at Bridget's following her around her garden at her painful pace, as she gasped at her Gauloises and swore at plants that weren't living up to her expectations. It was the slowness of her pace, as much as anything, that helped to sharpen his observation, and he would ask her, 'Is that a variegated *Polygonatum* you have there?'

She would take a last drag at her cigarette, and aim the stub at the plants in question with a stabbing throw, and say, 'Why? Don't you like it?'

Adam would say, 'I hate it. I prefer the original.'

'I can't stand it either,' Bridget would say, lighting another cigarette. 'I keep meaning to throw it out.'

When Adam reached the age of seventeen, and while his mother was dying, he applied for a job in a nursery in England, and got it. His new employers were somewhat taken aback when the subject of holidays came up, and they asked him when would he need to go home to Ireland for a visit. He answered, 'I expect I will have to go back for a few days for my mother's funeral.' He said it in a matter of fact way, and they hadn't known until that moment that his mother was ill, let alone dying. When the news came through that she had died, he went away quietly for four days, and when he returned resumed his work, without talking to anyone about what had happened, and as far as anyone could tell, without grieving.

He was fortunate in his employment, in that he worked for a small family nursery with an excellent, if somewhat esoteric, reputation, and in the four years he spent there he had time to learn his trade thoroughly. It was a period when others of his generation were threading safety-pins through their flesh and screaming about nihilism in instant rock groups; a phenomenon of which Adam, tucked away in the hills on the border of Herefordshire and Worcestershire, was unaware. James visited him once, with his hair orange and in spikes, and his legs chained together, and Adam had difficulty in recognising his own brother, and could think of nothing to say to him. The other people who were there noticed that while James was around Adam changed, became intractable and silent, and the moment his brother went away, Adam changed back into himself.

It was while he worked at the nursery that Adam met Joshua Goodlands for the first time. I don't know if that name rings a bell with you. You may remember that Goodlands was the name of the family who lived at Inverclachan, the place where Dougie

Millar was conceived. Joshua was a son of that house, and he and his brother Paul had been the ones sleeping in bedrooms by the back stairs the night Annie Millar sneaked Iain MacLeod into her room. Since that time Joshua had grown up and spent the correct amount of time contemplating in the Himalayas, and married an extraordinary creature called Jane, and settled in Herefordshire, where he had reached the age when people begin to think about their gardens, and visit nurseries in the way that they once visited record shops.

Joshua came into the nursery one day and said, 'I wonder if you sell bay trees?'

Adam hardly looked up from the labels he was writing out. He glanced at the knees of the customer to confirm what he had read into the voice. A rich hippy in rags. 'No,' he said.

'Rowan trees?' Joshua persisted.

Adam had to look up this time. 'We don't sell trees,' he said.

'It's not for me,' Joshua said. 'It's for my wife. Sibyls used to chew on bay leaves, apparently, and fairies roost in rowans.'

It was unlikely, after such an introduction, that Adam should have struck up a friendship with Joshua Goodlands; but that had more to do with Norah Brennan, and wasn't until a year or two later.

Just as he was thinking that he had served his apprenticeship, and should be starting a business of his own, one of his employers died, and the other one offered Adam a partnership, which would in effect allow his own retirement. Adam was not yet twenty-two years old, but he had already proved himself capable of managing a business, and proved also that he had enough imagination to expand it. He indulged his interest in unusual herbaceous perennials; and in the older species of them rather than the newer hybrids. Fortunately, at about the same time, there was a revival in the fashion for these plants, and after five years he was employing six people and showing at the Chelsea Flower Show. He had a specialist knowledge of plants that grew in the shade, which went back to his days in the dark garden at Williamstown; and he began to write small pieces for the gardening journals on this and other subjects.

For those among you who enjoy such things, it is time for a love story. I am not going to bore you with an account of Adam's first love, as it is too abstract a notion to be dealt with here, and because auto-eroticism is not a subject that I have yet fully considered. Instead we will move straight on to the arrival in Herefordshire of a girl called Norah Brennan, who came there from her home in Switzerland, via the horticultural beau monde of Bavaria. Her parents were Irish. Her mother was a well-bred neurotic who had disgraced herself by marrying a wealthy meat-packer, after which the couple retired to live in the suburbs of Zurich, to be left alone in their simple adoration of each other. Growing up in an atmosphere of isolation, Norah, like Adam, found refuge among plants, but, unlike Adam, she received a formal education in the science and marketing of vegetable matter. She was a house guest of Joshua Goodlands in May 1980, and he asked Adam, with whom by now he had struck up a casual acquaintance, to come to supper so that she could have someone to talk to. Adam offered her a job at the nursery, not because he was in a position to employ her, but because he could think of no other way to keep the girl in his sights. If he hadn't, she would have returned to Switzerland the following week.

They were eating scrambled eggs on smoked salmon, because scrambled eggs was the only thing that Jane Goodlands could cook, and smoked salmon was the only way she could think of to make it respectable enough to feed dinner guests. Norah chain-smoked throughout the meal, but she and Adam were the only ones who refused the circulating reefers. After everyone else had left, and the Goodlands had gone to bed, Adam found that he was still sitting across the table from her, and although he had never considered himself funny, she was laughing at things he said, and so he began to ask her about herself, and she answered, in a voice that was perfectly English, but with a languorous Swiss drawl to it. 'I have finished with being a student. I am looking for a job.'

'What sort of job?' he said. He imagined, from her account of her training, that she would be off to do research for the United Nations or something.

'I don't know,' she said. 'It must be something interesting.'

He tried to do some quick calculations in his head, but he couldn't see that there was the money for another employee. He thought about sacking a man for her sake, but even from within infatuation he could see the madness of that. He had only met the girl five hours before. Then he had a flash of brilliance. He tilted his chair back, and balanced himself by holding on to the table, and said, 'Work for me. I can't afford to pay you. But you can work for a share of the profits.'

'What are the profits?' she said.

He said, 'That might depend on you.'

She said, 'I would like to see this nursery of yours.'

'Do,' he said. 'Any time.' He got to his feet, saying that he had to go, and she went to the door with him. They stood outside for a moment in the scent of magnolias in a night that was completely black. She pulled a goblet of magnolia towards her and held it beneath her nose.

He said, 'That is rather a coarse cultivar. I must persuade Joshua to get a better one.' She was a black shape outlined by the light from the hall, and he was standing as close to her as he decently could. 'I'm not much good at seducing people.' He was taking a gamble by saying it, because he couldn't see the expression on her face, but she raised her arm, and put her hand on his shoulder. He said, 'I suppose we could try kissing. If it's a disaster I'll just go home.'

She said, 'Shut up,' and he could feel the pressure of her hand on the back of his neck, pushing his head down towards her own.

After they had been kissing a long time, he said, 'I've been wondering all night what that would be like.'

She told him that he talked too much, and she kissed him again. She went back to the nursery with him that night, and slept with him, and slept with him almost every night for the following ten years.

34

From the first evening that he made love to her there was a fluidity and a compatibility to it that Adam had not experienced before. Afterwards, he often marvelled at the convenience of their relationship. That he should, on first sight, have fallen in love with a girl who shared his main interest in life; that things should have fallen into place so easily from the beginning. In the morning he woke before she did, with her body gathered into him, and he felt as comfortable as if she was a part of him that had been returned to him.

When she woke, he said to her, 'I don't believe in love, but if I had to choose one position to be locked into for the rest of my life, it would be this one.' And that was the moment that she began to fall in love with him.

The effect she had on his life was stunning. Apart from her horticultural knowledge, it turned out that she had a great talent for business management. She could keep books and handle employees and talk to bank managers. These were aspects of Adam's life that had been a strain to him until then, and he gladly relinquished responsibility for them, so that he could get on with the things he considered important: the plants themselves. He used to think sometimes that seducing her was the shrewdest business move he had ever made. It did not occur to him that it was she who had done the seducing.

In the life that they began together there was little need for conversation. Anything that needed to be said could be conveyed in terse telegrammatic sentences, half in Latin. When they were alone together, there would be a great flow of words from her, which he would listen to as an abstract sound, for the pleasure of hearing the sound of her voice. Sometimes, in the mornings, he would wake up singing in his sleep. It took a great effort of will on his part not to become self-conscious and fall silent once he began to awake; and to continue the song while he opened his eyes. Sometimes the song would be lost in the effort of waking up, but, if he could sustain it, the happiness that had spawned the song in his sleep would stay with him for the morning. And so in later years, she had a memory of waking up often to the tuneless sound of his voice and the sight of his naked torso bolt upright in the bed, and his gardener's right-hand plucking at the pillow beside her head. And it was his tendency towards this sort of behaviour, among other things, that led her to become lost in her love for him.

He agreed to marry her on condition that they did it without telling anyone, quietly, abroad. At first, these terms were too harsh for her, but by the Christmas of the year in which they met, she had begun to see them in a romantic light, and she arranged a secret wedding in Venice in the wintertime, with just the two of them and Monteverdi, and afterwards they walked about, and stood on the bridges and laughed at the sour people in gondolas. Although she agreed to laugh at the gondolas rather than sit in one, she developed a fixation that he should kiss her on the middle of a certain bridge between their hotel and the Academia. For four days he refused, rushing across that bridge whenever they came to it as if it was about to collapse; but on the last evening they spent there he was drunk and she persuaded him. He looked up and down the canal to make sure that no one was watching, and pecked her quickly on the cheek. Then he caught her arm and dragged her back to the hotel at a half-run, keeping to the shadows and glancing behind him.

With Norah's management of things, it wasn't long before they had bought-out the old owner of the nursery. And then the gardening boom of the late-eighties meant a huge expansion of their business. In particular there was a craze for hostas that the Parnell nursery was in a position to supply, hostas being one of Adam's pet subjects. Norah became interested in micropropagation, and under her influence the nursery was made technologically efficient and streamlined. They were able to expand their list to include plants that had been difficult to propagate by traditional methods. He put a great deal of effort into their own private garden, and, although he was fanatical about collecting any plant that he admired, his sense of overall design was sensible enough for them to be able to open their garden to the public in 1986. After that, he preferred to be in the garden in the evenings only, when it was empty of strangers. While he enjoyed overhearing their remarks and answering their questions in the sales area of the nursery, it hurt him to be exposed to any but the deeply initiated when he was with his personal collection.

They did not become rich, but money ceased to be a real worry. Norah would get into a state about their finances now and again, and have hysterics because a light had been left on unnecessarily. At these times Adam would become more silent than usual, because money bored him as a subject, and as long as there seemed to be enough of it he was happy not to think about it. Norah knew this, and so perhaps her hysterics were an attempt to get fiscal reality through to him. She couldn't see why she should be the only one who was prepared to spend the morning on the telephone finding the cheapest car insurance. If it were up to him he would buy the first policy offered and spend the morning at the cuttings bench.

It may have been that the wealth of her background gave her a different attitude to these matters. Once, they had arranged to go to an opera in Birmingham with the Goodlands, but Jane was ill and so there were only three of them. Norah and Joshua stood in the foyer of the theatre, touting the spare ticket until after the bell had rung, while Adam marched around impatiently, hissing at them every time he passed close by that they were going to miss the first act. But Norah hung on, standing in front of a pillar in her evening clothes with the ticket held out in front of her. And when she did find a buyer at the last moment, she haggled with him, and came away from the engagement looking as vindicated as if the ten or fifteen pounds that she had saved Joshua were a Gainsborough that she had rescued from a junk shop.

They never had children, which bothered Norah, because she thought that Adam must want them, despite what he said. Adam declared that he had no interest in being a parent. As if it was a joke, he said that he wasn't qualified for fatherhood, and that he preferred plants to people in any case. He told Norah that he put contentment before happiness.

That was odd, perhaps bizarre, and so, did he ever love her? One day, as he was watching her standing in the beds of *Paeonia mlokosewitscii* while they were all in flower, and he felt the lust creep over him that he always felt while he was watching her, at the same time he felt an aesthetic excitement shoot through him at the sight of the pale-yellow flowers and the pale leaves, and he thought that life might be perfect if only one could fuck flowers, or if peonies could give him an erection. It was a thought that disturbed the order of his mind for one moment but no more, and then he walked up behind Norah and kissed her on the neck behind the collar. Because it was Tuesday morning they were alone and could make love among the peonies. She fetched a raincoat from a nearby shed and placed it carefully between the rows, and she thought it was perfect, making love with the sunshine poking through the leaves and the flowers, with the scent of lilac on the air.

As soon as he began he knew it had been a mistake. Sex had never seemed so ugly an act to him as when he did it in the shadow of *Paeonia mlokosewitscii*. What had been an act of love until then became something crude and pornographic. He closed his eyes, because if he glanced up at the flowers the contrast between their beauty and the ugliness he was creating was too great. He wanted it to be over quickly, but his discomfort delayed his climax. He became conscious of how offensive his buttocks must look, and stopped to drag his jeans back over them so that they were covered. Norah mistakenly thought that this action was erotically catalytic in intention, and redoubled her efforts. He hissed at her to be careful of the plants, and pinned her legs down with his own in case she should do any damage. The constriction finished her off, and he had to put his hand over her mouth in case anyone walking past on the road should hear her. Then he faked an orgasm and looked about him to see where he had put down his weeding knife.

That was the beginning of the first rift in their marriage, because on fine Tuesday mornings after that Norah would come and find him in the garden and want to make love among *Arum creticum* or something equally brief and esoteric, and he would say that he didn't want to, and when she asked him why, he would say that he didn't like it, and she would say, 'You used to. We used to do it and you liked it.' And he would become exasperated and say, 'Once. Once isn't used to.' He took to making love to her twice on Monday nights so that he would have an excuse not to do it on Tuesday mornings, and it was impossible for him to explain to her, the object of his love, what sort of nightmare love among the peonies had been.

After Venice, they developed the habit of going away in the winter, of travelling to some place of botanic interest while there was not much to do in their own garden. By the time they were doing well they could afford to spend a month a year at this, culminating in a trip to China in February 1988. China was perhaps the main reason why they came to Inverclachan the following year.

It had always been Norah who was the driving force behind their trips abroad, because Adam thought that he was happy nowhere but at home, and he hated to miss the blooming of a single flower in his garden, even if there was nothing out but the viburnums and the odd Algerian iris. And he thought, too, that Norah's personality changed when they were abroad, and he liked her less out of context; but it wasn't until after China, where they had been given stir-fried kittens to eat on the Yellow River, that he felt that he had reason to put his foot down and stay home the following year.

So Inverclachan was a sort of compromise. Norah agreed not to go abroad, but insisted that he get away from the nursery for a while. They had been to Inverclachan once or twice before, to spend the weekend with Joshua and Jane, who had retained the cottage below the flagpole for holidays and the use of their friends. The estate itself was run by Joshua's older brother Paul, who was a permanent resident at Inverclachan, in the drier rooms of the big house. Joshua Goodlands offered his cottage to the Parnells at a modest rent for six weeks around Christmas and the New Year, and Norah accepted, and Adam, thinking that anything would be better than China, agreed.

The cottage that Joshua let them was half-way up the gully that led to the flagpole. It was a long low house surrounded by oak trees and pockets of bog, with a view over the seaward end of the loch and out to the Western Isles. Adam had said on a previous visit that it was the most relaxing place that he knew, because the landscape was unimprovable: it was the only place he had been to that foiled his neurosis to plant things.

Adam and Norah arrived on a dark wet evening. A ferryboat, blazing with light, passed down the loch below the house, and the air was full of the sinister noises of an unidentifiable seabird. When they went into the house they discovered that someone had lit a fire for them, and left a saucepan of soup that only needed to be warmed. They didn't know it, but that was the work of Dougie and Jean Millar, who had been commissioned by Joshua to clean the house for their arrival.

Dougie Millar, who lived at Shore Cottage by this time, and had his gossip second- or third-hand, had heard that an Irish poet called Parnell was coming to live at Inverclachan, and he was looking forward to meeting him. He had romantic ideas about the Irish and about poets and surnames like Parnell. He spent longer than he should have in Joshua's cottage, straightening the books on the shelves, and pulling the volumes that he thought an Irish poet would enjoy into more prominent positions, and when Jean had finished everything that she could do, he let her walk back to Shore Cottage on her own, while he settled down in front of the fire he had just lit, and rolled a cigarette. He let his imagination run to evenings of verse and nationalism, and when he finally left the house he left his matches behind, because there were none in the place otherwise. Back at home, he listened to the sound of the odd car passing the cottage until he heard an engine that was unfamiliar and then he knew that they had arrived.

About three days before Christmas, Adam and Norah had walked out to Glen Dubh and back. It was a still, bright day and they had a fight as they came home, so that by the time they reached the cottage Adam was fifty paces ahead of Norah. While their life at the nursery was one of uninterrupted harmony, they often fought on holiday. It was usually over something trivial, and usually, while it lasted, they hated each other.

As he came up the hill, Adam saw that there was a tractor stuck in the ditch outside the cottage with Paul Goodlands sitting on it. He was trying to drive it out of the ditch, but only succeeding in throwing up clods of mud and wild irises, at the same time as digging the tractor in deeper. Adam stopped and asked if he could help, and Paul switched the engine off and climbed down to him. They were both gazing into the ditch when Norah came up to them, and Adam was saying, in an authoritative voice, 'You will have to get the other tractor to pull it out.' He found that Paul Goodlands, with his public-school confidence, had that effect on him, and his only defence against Paul's version of charm was a strident voice. Paul's presence made him feel awkward, and he disliked the man for it.

As Norah approached, Paul turned to her with an ex-hippy grin stretched across his face, and said, 'Hi.'

Norah, who had known Paul for many years before she knew Adam, smiled at him, and said, 'You don't have to take any notice of Adam, you know. He thinks he knows everything.' She said it as if it was a joke, so that she could carry on fighting with Adam without compromising Paul.

Adam ignored her, and offered Paul a lift back to the farm, but Paul said that he would be as quick cutting across the hill.

After he was gone, Norah said, 'Why do you have to do that? Why do you have to be the expert?'

He said, 'I do know something about tractors.'

'It isn't that,' she said. 'It's the way you say it.'

He said, 'What? I should learn to be as charming and self-deprecating as Paul? Yuch. Anyway, you can only carry off those kind of manners if you've been to public school. It's only a sort of institutionalised arrogance.'

'How would you know?' she said.

He said, 'Perhaps you should have married an old Etonian.'

'This is stupid,' she said. 'Can we start again?' She put her arms around him.

'That's up to you,' he said. 'You started the fight.'

She said that she hated him sometimes, but she was trying to kiss him. And he said that he could believe it, but the fight was over, and they settled back into their normal state.

'I love you terribly,' she said.

'Exactly,' he said.

Norah went back into the house, and Adam stayed outside, waiting for the other tractor to come. He was still irritated to some degree by Norah's criticism of his manners. He knew that somewhere beneath her love for him she was capable of snobbery, because he had seen it in her parents, and their pathetic efforts to be careless of social values: the way her mother had seemed so down to earth, but at the same time he saw her run his surname through a mental list of people whom one could know in Ireland; and how she had irritated him by telling humorous stories in a terrible brogue, and how her husband, the meat-packer, had gone along with it because he was used to being patronised, and because he was nearly dead anyway. It was only after he died that she returned to Ireland, to find that her husband's sort of people were the new ascendancy, and they need never have run away in the first place. She settled in England to be near her daughter, and to play bridge with a horde of like-minded crones who honestly believed sometimes that they were still living in the hills around Simla or the villas behind Greystones. Norah, of course, was not to be blamed for any of this, but Adam did wonder what sort of coincidence it was that all her friends were the sort of people her mother would have approved of, except for himself; and even he was hardly what you might call a bit of rough. The one time he mentioned this to Norah, she said that they were all people she had known for years, and how could he understand it, since he himself had no friends at all?

When Paul returned, driving the other tractor, he had two men standing on the back of it. One of them was Craig Anderson, the Inverclachan shepherd, a shambling, sensible man who was happier speaking Gaelic than English, to such a degree that most of the time it was hard to tell which tongue he was using. The other man was Dougie Millar.

Dougie Millar had grown up to be an exact reproduction of Iain MacLeod. He was three inches over six feet, and he had the miserable eyes, and the lipless mouth, and the tight skin and black hair of his father. If he had an air of belonging to another world, it was maybe to do with having lived eight years already beyond the age at which his father had hanged himself, and he felt that the time was stolen and he had no right to be there. He disguised his reactions with such skill that you would never have known, by watching him, the closeness and eagerness with which he was inspecting Adam. Indeed, Adam didn't notice him looking in his direction once.

Despite behaving like the team leader in an Army initiative test, Paul was hopelessly incompetent. It was only the quiet wisdom of the two Scotsmen that prevented him from losing the second tractor. Because of the contrast with the other two men, Adam saw Paul in a new, and rather physical, light, and realised for the first time how ugly the man was. Until then, because Paul had the self-confidence of someone who was good-looking, Adam had assumed that he must be. But as the situation with the tractors deteriorated, the self-confidence vanished, and Adam saw a small, red-faced man, with bulging eyes and a tilted nose, and hands that were like pink-skinned potatoes, who dashed between the other two, making a spectacle of himself. Dougie and Craig said very little, but caught each other's eye from time to time over the head of the other man. Adam tried to be in on the conspiracy, but Dougie seemed unaware of him, and he had to make do with the odd cryptic joke from Craig Anderson. At least, he assumed that they were jokes, since Craig didn't take offence when he laughed at them.

Dougie Millar was badly disappointed with Adam. Having expected a sort of Brendan Behan, he found instead a perfectly sober man who spoke the same sort of colonial English as the Goodlands. And Adam was not at all soulful, but quite energetic, and smiled to himself all the time. And he looked nothing like any of the tragic likenesses of Charles Stewart Parnell. Dougie decided to forget the whole thing, that there was nothing to be salvaged from it, and after the salvation of the tractor, he declined the general offer of a dram with a shake of his head. Adam saw nothing more of him until New Year's Eve.

An unspeakable couple called Tim and Judy de Buis came over from France to spend Hogmanay with the Parnells. They were friends of Norah's from her youth, and although Adam could find nothing specific to object to in either of them, he was usually careful, in a tactful way, not to be left alone in a room with them. They were not easy guests. Judy took over the cooking, and Tim made a big thing about going into Achacloaigh for what he called a carload of drink, even though Adam said that there was plenty of drink in the house already. In the event, Tim's carload of drink turned out to be a case of the cheapest whisky imaginable. The de Buis snickered about the primitive standard of the shops in Achacloaigh and Tim complained that there wasn't a bottle of Grand Cru-anything to be had in the entire town. 'Bulgarian wine. Imagine? What on earth do people drink here?'

'Not this,' Adam said, holding up a bottle of the whisky they had bought.

Norah warned him off with a look, and the de Buis pretended to be too worldly to know what he was talking about. In desperation, on New Year's Eve, Adam suggested that they should all go first-footing, but of course Tim insisted that they bring a bottle of that whisky with them. They set off across the hill towards the farm as soon as midnight had struck. Craig Anderson, who lived at the farm, opened the door to them, and eyed the bottle in Tim's hand, and said, 'I buy Grouse myself. I find it's worth the money. Happy New Year to you.'

The atmosphere at the farm was difficult. Neither the de Buis nor Norah could understand the Andersons' accents, and anything they said had to be repeated several times, and there was a suspicion that perhaps the Andersons would prefer to be watching their telly. After half an hour, Judy said that she was sick, which as she was mildly pregnant at the time was excusable, and Tim offered to take her back, and Norah said that she was tired and would go with them.

Adam, given the chance of escaping from the de Buis, said that he would carry on with the first-footing. As he was half-way out the door, Craig came after him with the untouched de Buis whisky, saying, 'Here, don't forget your bottle.'

Adam said, 'I was hoping I could.'

The next house he had to pass was the big house, and Adam stood outside it for a minute or two, wondering whether to call in, but there was something about the atmosphere between Paul and his wife Lucinda that dissuaded him, and there was something about the look of the house that suggested they might be in bed already. He decided to press on and try his luck at Shore Cottage instead. Dougie answered the door to him, and Adam apologised as he entered. 'This is terrible. I forgot the coal, and the whisky I have with me is an abomination; but it's not my fault.' He took the bottle out of his pocket and handed it to Dougie.

'I think we can do better than that,' Dougie said. 'Sit down.'

Jean was sitting in front of a blazing fire. She and Dougie were wearing their best, and the kitchen table was spread with drink and sausage rolls. Once he was sitting down, Adam could think of nothing to say, and began to feel uncomfortable. He realised that he was not used to going to other people's houses on his own. If Norah had been with him, she would have found something to exclaim over by now. She would be telling the Millars how lucky they were to be living at Inverclachan all the time; asking questions about the children and drooling politely over their photographs.

Dougie handed Adam a glass full of whisky, and Adam said, 'Am I the first?'

Jean said, 'Ay. And you're tall and dark. You'll do.'

'Not handsome?'

Jean said, 'You'll do.'

Adam thought he heard a snort of amusement from Dougie, who was standing behind him, but when he turned Dougie's face was impassive. Adam said, 'I was just up at the farm.'

'How was that?' Jean said.

'Quite good. Craig got very sentimental towards the end. We were talking in Gaelic, and he told me that his favourite song was "A Mother's Love's a Blessing". I think he wanted to sing it to me, but Moira stopped him.'

Jean was smiling at that, and Dougie had come round to sit across the fire from him.

Dougie said, 'You speak Gaelic?'

Adam said, 'You have to learn it if you go to school in Ireland. I've forgotten most of it.' He had the impression that Dougie seemed to be a little bit relaxed and reassured by that, but he couldn't think why he should be.

Dougie said, 'So, you're a poet, I hear.'

Adam stretched his neck with the shock of it, but before he could form a denial Jean said, 'No. I told you he was a writer. Lucinda said he wrote for garden magazines.'

Adam said, 'I'm not that either. I'm a gardener.' He could detect a cynical cast crossing Dougie's face. He felt that he was losing the man's approval again. It irritated him to think that he was worrying about whether Dougie approved of him or not. He said, 'I have a nursery. Norah and I have a nursery in England. Do you know England at all?'

Dougie said, 'I worked down there once. I didn't like it.'

A few moments of silence followed. Adam said, 'Un ange passe,' and then regretted saying it, because it was the sort of pretentious thing the de Buis would have said to show off, but neither Dougie nor Jean seemed to have noticed it, and the silence continued. The strange thing was that the silence was good-humoured, and its effect was to make Adam relax and look about himself. There was a wedding photograph on top of the television. The Millars were barely recognisable in it, got up in the height of early-seventies fashion. Jean in a smock and platforms, and Dougie wearing a tie four inches wide, with his hair permed and parted in the middle and down to his shoulders. Adam laughed out loud. 'Was that you?'

'Ay,' Dougie said.

Adam said, 'I remember hair like that. I always knew that if I kept my hair short the world would come back to its senses. My brother was thrown out of school for having hair like that. Although maybe I only kept mine short to be different from him. We didn't like each other too much. Or maybe he grew his long to be different from me. I never thought of that.' He looked at the photograph closely and then he looked at the Millars, and said, 'You must have married young.'

'Seventeen,' Dougie said.

46

Jean said, 'We were both seventeen.'

'Children,' Adam said.

Dougie said, 'Ay.'

Jean said, 'So how do you like living up here?'

'Wonderful,' Adam said. Then he looked at both of them as if he was going to take a risk, and said, 'I don't know how Orange you all are or anything; or whether that sort of thing still applies here, but one thing really bugs me. I was never political: I could never get interested in republicanism when I lived in Ireland; but I suppose you never appreciate what you have. It gets under my skin that the English are still in charge here. It is only now that I can see what independence was all about. The English are a wonderful people; don't get me wrong. I make a good living there doing something I could never have got away with in Ireland; but while I am here I just keep thinking that the people in this country are too intelligent to be ruled by them. You can't apply one set of rules to two peoples who are so different. Red post-boxes in Scotland get my goat. And the signs on the motorway that go on saying "the north", as if the border didn't exist, or this wasn't a separate country.'

Adam realised that he had been leaning forward with earnestness while he was talking, and collapsed back into his chair. Dougie stood up and came towards him, and Adam wondered what was going to happen.

Dougie said, 'I think you better have another dram,' and took the glass out of Adam's hand.

Adam said, 'You can give me the stuff I brought, if you want.'

Dougie said, 'I wouldn't even give that to an Englishman.'

Adam said, 'So you're a nationalist.'

'Of course,' Dougie said. 'Anyone with a pair of eyes and a brain is a nationalist.'

'The Goodlands aren't,' Adam said.

Dougie said nothing, only raised an eyebrow and snorted. But that was eloquent enough, and Jean said, 'So what do you think of Inverclachan then?'

Adam realised that he was on the verge of another long bout of speech, and took a gulp of whisky. He was enjoying listening to himself, because the sound of his own voice was a novelty to him. Usually he was grateful to let Norah do the talking. 'Wonderful,' he said. 'Inverclachan is anti-gardening. It makes people like me redundant. If the rest of the world were like Inverclachan there would be no need to fiddle with it and plant things. Do you know that place out by Glen Dubh, with big chunks of rectangular rock thrown around and covered in moss, and the sunlight coming through the trunks of the birches? I was thinking the other day that if you were a Japanese gardener in the fourteenth century, if you were Mūso Soseki himself, you could spend your whole life rearranging stones and plants and not come up with something as good as that. This is the only place I could retire to if I wanted to give up gardening.'

He thought, as he was speaking, that if he had been saying these things a half an hour before, he would have embarrassed himself, but something had changed in the atmosphere since then. There were times when he almost thought that Dougie was smiling at him, and the conversation went on, quietly and naturally, for another hour or so, and when Adam walked home, he was a little drunk, and singing to himself.

As the new year settled in, Lucinda Goodlands began to develop the habit, on fine days, of calling on Adam and Norah in the middle of the morning. She would come in with her squad of precocious children and wet dogs, and remove perhaps half of the layers of her outer clothes, and settle herself in the middle of their kitchen, where she simultaneously rolled a very small cigarette and pulled up her jersey to breastfeed a baby. She had one of those small fine faces which had been considered pretty while she was young and living in London; and still was pretty, except that in the intervening fifteen years in the Highlands she had forgotten how to apply make-up properly, and she was so thin that you wondered how she could possibly have any milk for the baby, which spent most of its day dangling from one nipple or the other when it wasn't wailing with hunger. Her other children and her dogs wandered about the house, looking for breakable things to play with and demanding orange squash.

If Adam was there when Lucinda called, she only talked about money; investments and shares and how lucky she was that Black Monday had left her relatively unscathed. It was a conversation that Lucinda could easily have held with herself, but as it was, she seemed to require the odd nod of the head from her audience in between bouts of repeating the same facts, figures and projections. After half an hour or so of that, Adam would wander out of the room as if he had something to do, and once she was alone with Norah, Lucinda could turn the conversation to the subject that really motivated her visits.

It would seem, on certain days, that Paul was having an affair, with an old and landed flame of his; and on other days it would seem that Paul was a paragon who would be incapable of such a thing. Lucinda presented a daily litany of her marriage to Norah that was superficially not unlike the litany of her finances; except that with money her general tone was self-congratulatory, while marriage, even when it was good, was inclined to make her despair. It would seem that Paul Goodlands was not an easy man to live with. He had spent the entire previous winter in bed with a bout of depression; and this winter was plagued by an insomnia, because of which he spent his nights wandering about the estate and sitting on clifftops. 'Well,' Lucinda said, 'I suppose it is better than when we were spending all of every night screaming at each other.'

To begin with, Norah was a good listener. Because she had known Paul for a long time, when she was able to get a word in, she could offer small amounts of good advice; and because of her goodness, she was able to believe whatever she was told at its face value, so that when she repeated Lucinda's confidences to Adam, she could do so sympathetically and without a trace of cynicism. In spite of this, she came to dread the visits (while remaining fond of the woman herself), and there came a day when, at the sight of the first sodden dog slinking through the door, heralding the arrival of Lucinda's entourage, Norah made a dash for the other end of the house, telling Adam to say that she had gone out for a walk. It was beyond Adam to tell a lie that would be so easily discovered, since he knew that within minutes one of the roaming children would have found Norah in her hiding place, and so he made no reference to her at all, but offered Lucinda tea in the usual way, and settled down to hear about the buoyancy of the Hong Kong stock market.

It seemed to Adam that Lucinda was more agitated than usual, because she left the baby to roar in a pram outside and flung herself dramatically into a seat without removing any of her coats, saying, 'Disaster!' She tried to run her fingers up through her hair, but since she hadn't brushed it in more than a fortnight, they stuck at the nape of her neck. It was only then that she noticed Norah's absence and asked where she was.

'Ahm,' Adam said. 'I'm not sure.' There was a distant noise of children hammering on the door of the bathroom where Norah had closeted herself. 'I think,' he said, 'she might be coming.' He had taken to playing games with Lucinda; hanging about longer than was necessary, to see how long she would last before the subject of her husband came to the surface, despite Adam's presence.

Norah appeared in the room, silently, so that she could shoot a dirty look at Adam before she was seen by Lucinda.

'Lucinda has had a disaster,' Adam said.

Norah said, 'Oh dear. What is it?' She could only imagine that Paul had finally run off with the landed flame.

'Jean is pregnant,' Lucinda said.

Both Adam and Norah were silent for a moment while they remembered who Jean was, and then Norah said, 'That's terrible. She must have enough to do with the two she has.' Adam thought of Dougie, and said, 'Did they mean to have it, or not?'

Lucinda looked from one of them to the other, puzzled, as though these were aspects of the situation which hadn't occurred to her, and said, 'No, it's a disaster for me. Who's going to do my housework?'

Norah said, 'That won't be for months yet.' She had said it automatically, but as soon as she had she regretted it and looked at Adam. He had been about to fill the teapot, but without a word or change of expression he put the kettle down and left the room.

It was three hours before he returned, and Norah was looking out for him. She ran and threw her arms around him, and said that she was sorry, darling.

'Is that woman gone?' he said.

Norah said, 'She isn't so bad. She doesn't mean it.'

'Oh, I know,' Adam said. 'She can blame stupidity. What's your excuse?'

'I said I was sorry.'

'Sorry,' Adam said. 'I've just spent three hours kicking boulders and thinking of sarcastic things to say. It seemed a waste not to say one of them. Do you want to hear the rest?'

That was the last of Lucinda's visits that Adam was aware of, because in the few days that remained to them at Inverclachan, he made sure that he was out of the house in the morning, and, if she did visit after that, he missed her. He spent his mornings walking about the estate, trying to fix Inverclachan in his mind, thinking that being there was an experience he wouldn't repeat, and so he found himself looking more closely at the place than he had before. These walks were solitary, and at first, when he saw something that was extraordinary, he had an automatic urge to turn to someone and point it out; and as no one was there, he saved sentences to tell Norah when he returned, and to begin with, when he saw her again, he would trot them out like a child back from school. Later on, keeping the sentences to himself was not a deliberate act: bit by bit, he found that he had difficulty remembering them when faced with Norah, and by the time he recalled them the recounting seemed unimportant. And then he began to look at things without bothering to form sentences, and found that his impressions were less spoiled for being left visual and not put into words.

They left Scotland in a terrible storm. Norah was sentimental about leaving: she swore eternal friendship at their goodbyes, even to the woman in the vegetable shop in Achacloaigh. Adam was not a man for goodbyes; he stood impatiently in the background; but as they drove along the shore to leave Inverclachan he saw Dougie walking towards them, bent into the storm with a shovel over his shoulder. He hadn't seen him since the New Year, and he waved to him, and Dougie raised his head in the rain and waved back, and afterwards, Adam remembered thinking that if you had to say goodbye that was the way to do it.

On the motorway somewhere in Lancashire, the clutch went in the car, and because they were on the motorway it cost a fortune to have it mended, and Norah said, 'Why aren't we in the AA? I have to be back tonight. I have a meeting at the bank tomorrow.'

And he said, 'Don't worry. We'll get you there.'

She said, 'I knew something like this would happen.'

And he said, 'Don't shout. You can't pin this one on me. There is no reason why you couldn't have thought of joining the AA yourself.'

She said, 'Well, you do what you like. I have to be at that meeting.'

And he thought that these were the worst moments. In any crisis she was always blindly scrambling for the exit. He wished that they could avoid crises so that he never had to see her like this, but meanwhile he telephoned for a taxi to take her to the nearest train station so that she could get to her meeting, and he stayed with the car. After she was gone, he thought that, if anything, he rather enjoyed this sort of crisis; to be stuck for a few hours at an anonymous service station in an unfamiliar landscape. After she was gone he could relax and look around him.

The business was expanding. That spring they employed a propagation manager for the first time, and the packing operation was made completely independent of the rest of the nursery. It was all organised and financed and overseen by Norah. That left Adam with more time to consider his lists and his garden, but he did wonder, once or twice, what there would be left for him to do the following winter. Although orders were at a record level, the new processes excluded him, and it began to seem that his own nursery had outgrown him.

Norah said, 'We could go away for even longer next year. Maybe a half-sabbatical.'

'Where?' he said.

She said, 'Inverclachan was pretty good.'

'We've done that,' he said.

She said, 'I wouldn't mind going back.'

He said, 'It never pays to repeat a success.'

And the subject was dropped. But sometime in March – do you know that first hot day of the year, when you take your shirt off and walk about grinning, because after a long winter that is what the sun will do to you? – it was a Tuesday and they were alone. Adam had been transplanting white foxgloves, and when he had finished he went to find Norah in the micropropagation unit. She was bent over her sterile bench, with a scalpel in each hand, slicing a callous. He said, 'Where do you want to go for lunch?'

She said nothing for a moment, and then she turned towards him and said, 'If we organised it properly, we could have a child sometime next winter.' If there was something menacing in her manner, it

53

might have been because she was still holding the scalpels in her plastic-coated hands, and her glasses were still on her nose and her hair in a plastic shower cap.

Adam said, 'Why?'

They went to a place where they went often, by the river, where they could sit out. But as soon as they got there they both regretted that they hadn't stayed at home to eat in their own garden, and to make themselves feel better they ordered lobster and the most expensive wine on the menu, which was only a Pouillé fuissé, but not bad. Before the food had come, the sky began to cloud over and a cold wind came off the river. They went inside and ate with spring rain driving against the windows.

Adam noticed that Norah wasn't really eating, although she was putting away the wine as fast as he could pour it. He felt that he couldn't ask her what the matter was, because he had a feeling that she might cry. He hoped that she mightn't cry before he had finished his lobster, because emotions spoil good food so easily. Even so, his anticipation of her outburst had spoiled the food, and so there was perhaps a touch of impatience in his voice when he did ask her what the matter was.

As he had predicted, tears came streaming out of her eyes before he had finished the sentence.

'You won't even talk about it,' she said. 'Why shouldn't we have a baby?'

The place was almost empty, and what people there were were behind Norah's back, so he thought that if he spoke in a normal tone of voice no one would take any notice of them. 'Is that what you really want?' he said. 'You want to be another Lucinda Goodlands, traipsing around with some pink alien hanging from your tit, so hamstrung that you have nothing else to do all day but worry about your husband's state of mind?'

'Why?' she said. 'What is wrong with having a child?'

And he said, 'Nothing. But we are happy as we are. And what is so great about us that we are fit to inflict ourselves on children? Parents are unforgivable. Plants are more forgiving than children. I think we had better leave, don't you?' He had run out of things he could say in a quiet polite voice. He got up from the table and went to pay the bill.

The rain turned into a downpour as they drove back. As they

approached the house he exploded, and said, 'Oh, for Christ's sake, if you want a child, you can have a child. But don't expect me to have anything to do with it. If I wanted to change my life in any way, I wouldn't change it so that I was more tied down than I am.'

She said, 'You feel tied down?'

He said, 'That wasn't what I said. Don't push it.'

That was the day that they first noticed the crack in the kitchen wall had grown larger. They had opened a bottle of wine to oil the wheels of reconciliation, and they were both leaning against the Aga rail, and Norah said, 'Had you noticed that crack before?' On the wall opposite there was a thin black line, about three and a half feet long. Adam said yes and then he said no, because he could remember that there was a crack, but not such a big one. He made a pencil mark at the top and bottom of it, and they watched it for a while, as though they expected it to grow before their eyes.

Later, when Adam was a little drunk, he said to her, 'I have nothing to give to children. I am someone who hasn't yet got over his own childhood. What kind of father could I be?'

He was surprised to hear himself say that, and the next day, when he remembered it, he wondered what he could have meant by it. In the end he decided that he had spoken out of expediency, as an excuse for not wanting to be burdened with children; as an excuse for his own selfishness. He pushed it away to the back of his mind, and for a while he managed to forget that he had said it.

The crack, on the other hand, grew larger. Within a week it had grown a foot, and they began to notice other cracks about the house. Eventually they got in a surveyor, who said that the house was sliding down the hill towards the brook, and that it needed major structural work.

Norah said, 'I don't want to live on a building site for three months. Why don't we have it done in the winter, while we are at Inverclachan?'

Adam said, 'I wasn't aware that we were going to Inverclachan.'

'Well, it's obvious.' She stopped speaking for a moment while she considered her next sentence. 'You said yourself there would be nothing for us to do here this winter. We could have a proper long holiday. Three or four months. It isn't so far away that one of us couldn't come back from time to time.'

Adam said, 'I give up.' Then he said, 'No, I don't. We'll see.'

That summer was busy for them, and the subject of children was dropped. Norah thought it was better that she didn't tell Adam she had had her coil removed in the spring, hoping that the child would be born in January or February, when she meant them to be at Inverclachan. As the summer progressed she began to resign herself to the idea that the child would have to be born in England, but at least she would be pregnant at Inverclachan. She saw herself, standing huge with child, on the shore by the sea buckthorns.

Adam enjoyed his summer: being a shopkeeper, and standing among the rows in the nursery-sales area, overhearing the things that people said about him and his garden. One or two even recognised him, and one old woman asked him to autograph the label of the plant she was buying. It occurred to him once or twice that summer that he had cracked it; that he led as happy a life as anyone could reasonably expect; and he watched Norah, while she worked at her bench with her glasses on the end of her nose, and there was no particular thought in his head, but he could just stand there, unobserved, watching her and feeling contented.

BOOK TWO

Paul Goodlands came out of his office smiling to himself. He was having one of those unaccountable bouts of good humour that assailed him from time to time in his life. It was the first wet day of a dry September. He wanted to go somewhere quiet and smoke a joint; calm down a bit and get closer to the normal state that he was comfortable with. He walked the shore for a while, stopping to set alight the odd bit of washed-up plastic, listening to the drizzle hissing on the flames; and then he turned towards the flagpole. He had to pass Joshua's cottage on the way, which was full of holiday-makers. He debated going a longer way to avoid speaking to them, but decided that the risk was minimal in the rain. His luck held, and they never saw him pass. They were huddled inside around a portable television they had brought with them. He began to stretch his legs out and take the hill in even strides. The oaks were still green and the bracken long. Bracken was supposed to be carcinogenic at this time of year, but there was still pleasure in wading through it. There was a theory now that bracken should be eliminated like the rhododendrons, as an invasive species; and there was talk of a grant from the Nature Conservancy for doing it. Someone had said that they had found a parasite that would eat it all away. But Paul was fonder of bracken than he was of rhododendron: at the other end of the year he waited for it to unfurl as the first sure sign of summer.

When he came in sight of the flagpole, he saw that there was a figure by it already, sitting on a boulder with his back to the loch. Paul slowed and walked silently round to the side until he could see the face of whoever it was.

Dougie Millar had spotted Paul a long way down the hill, and had turned away so that the other might have the chance to pass without exchanging a greeting. He made use of his hands being in the lee of the rain to pull out his tobacco tin and start a roll-up. He was taking his first pull from it when Paul came and stood before him.

Paul said the word hi with a broad sociable smile, and Dougie said the word hello without one. Dougie also winced, involuntarily, but he made it look as though the wind had blown smoke into his eye.

'The dry was too good to last,' Paul said.

Dougie said ay.

Paul sat down on the next boulder along and took out his own tobacco box. He unwrapped the dope from a bit of plastic and began to burn the end with his lighter. He put the burning lump to his lips and inhaled sharply. The rain was easing away and there was sunshine out over the Islands, coming closer.

Paul nodded down the hill to Joshua's cottage. Between the trees you could make out the black roof, shining wet. 'The Parnells are coming back to Inverclachan for the winter,' he said.

There was something in what Paul said that threw Dougie off balance. He had been numb since Kerry's death. He resented the idea that Paul Goodlands had said the first thing to penetrate his numbness. But nothing showed on his face. He pinched out the lighted tip on his own cigarette and took the smoking joint from Paul's outstretched hand. He turned around on the boulder as if to look down at the cottage, but it really had more to do with turning his back on Paul.

He thought about Kerry to make himself numb again. The sea was turning blue in the sun, where the Islands floated on it, out to the west. They should have buried Kerry in the sparkling sea, not the acid leaking earth.

The funeral was maybe the worst part. It is unusual for women to attend funerals in Scotland, and so it is a man's job to bury his children. Dougie Millar had carried his own daughter's small coffin up the hill to where they were to bury her. There was a minister and an undertaker and himself; no one else. You can't expect crowds at your funeral if you've only lived for an hour. For most of the time Dougie thought that the only people present were the two professionals. He couldn't see himself there at all.

It was a powerful day. The sky was huge; the land immense; the sea looked endless. It was a day as banal as any other. There was nothing to separate it from other days, except that for the rest of his life Dougie would hold his hands out eighteen inches apart and see a coffin between them the size of a shoebox, and the toe-caps of his own feet appearing beneath it, one by one, as he walked up the hill to where they buried her.

If you have to be buried somewhere, it may be as well to be buried on a hillside overlooking the Western Isles: if you had to die. If you died when you were an hour old, would you know what a Western Isle was to appreciate it? Does scenery matter to the soul of an infant? And if not, why did they have to bury her at the top of a hill, so that afterwards, whenever you walked up to her, you were racked with tears before you were half-way there?

Going up the hill and coming down, Dougie Millar couldn't believe that he was there at all. Standing over the hole that they put her in, he thought that he was not standing, but floating. His body was in the black car below on the road end.

If there was any part of his body that was up by the grave, he thought that it might be his hands. Something had to bring the coffin up. He was thinking that perhaps he should leave his hands there in the grave with her, since they had had so much to do with her conception and her birth and her burial. He would have liked to leave his hands as a present for her, but already the other men were guiding him back down the hill to the car at the road end.

Jean cried for a week, without stopping. Some women do as much when they give birth to a child who lives, although perhaps not with that intensity, and Jean was not a woman who was normally given to crying. When she stopped, her ribs ached from the sobbing. Dougie did what he could to comfort her, but Kerry's death was between them: there could be no unity in the face of something as senseless. It was as well that the other children were back at school, but Dougie still had to keep things together in the evening. The television helped, because there was no need to talk once it was on. But in the days, while Jean cried in the bedroom, he found himself, not pacing, but wandering up and down, with his hands spaced eighteen inches apart, gazing into the gap between them. It was the nearest he could come to making sense of it.

They avoided people, because people could find nothing to say to them, and Dougie was glad that they lived at Inverclachan, because it was a place where you need never see anyone if you didn't want to. And on the other hand, the beauty of Inverclachan began to appal him. They had come to live there for idealistic reasons, and Kerry was to be the Inverclachan baby: the embodiment of the ideal. He developed an instinct, which told him that he should run away, not only from Inverclachan, but from Jean and the children.

Luckily, perhaps, while it lasted this instinct was not as strong as the numb torpor that had come over him with grief. He would not have been capable of doing anything new or different; he could barely go through the motions of doing the things that he knew well, and often he would do them without knowing what he had done. He would have to go back and feel his toothbrush to know if he had brushed his teeth.

After Jean came out of the worst of her misery, and the bed was empty in the mornings, he took to lying in, sometimes not getting up the whole day, or drawing the curtains. Jean told him that if he wasn't careful he would be as bad as Paul Goodlands, who had been known to spend a whole winter in his bed; but with Dougie it lasted ten days or so, in the beginning. And then one morning the weather changed and the drizzle came, and he found himself wandering out of the house towards the flagpole. He came the back way, by the farm, and Craig nodded to him from the yard but kept his distance.

Paul's joint was welcome enough, and there were aspects of Paul's company that were not as bad as the man himself. His caste consciousness meant that he expected no real answers when he spoke; it was beyond him to think that a man like Dougie could challenge the wisdom that dropped from his lips, and it suited Dougie to let the man go on thinking that. There are advantages, when in the company of people like Paul Goodlands, in being considered inarticulate, of no intellectual value. The chief advantage to Dougie was that he didn't have to pretend that anything the man said was worth listening to.

His remembrance of the funeral blotted out his awareness of Paul behind him, and when he turned away from the loch again Paul had gone, and he could see him in the distance crossing down the hill field towards the farm. Dougie stood up, finding that his knees had locked into position and his feet were asleep. He began to walk down the loch side of the hill on his dead feet, taking a sort of enjoyment in the pain of it, the sweet run of pins and needles on his soles. Outside Joshua's cottage he stopped, looking at the silhouette of heads before the television, and tried to remember what he could about the Parnells. He could see Adam's face by the fire at New Year, when Kerry was barely conceived, but because it came back to Kerry he could remember nothing more about the people. He walked on down the hill, and when he looked at his hands they were held out again eighteen inches apart.

Achacloaigh is a town that faces the wrong way for its own comfort. It is situated on the eastern side of an isthmus of hills that separates it from Inverclachan. And so, while Inverclachan gets the worst of the big storms, the ordinary rainclouds from the Atlantic pass straight over it and dump their load on the people of Achacloaigh. On almost any fine day in winter that you set out to do your shopping, you can be sure of rain in the small grey town, and if you raise your dripping head you will see a band of clear sky to the west where the sun is still shining at home.

Thursday was the best day for shopping in Achacloaigh because the place was stocked up for the weekend. If you came in on a Friday or a Saturday the place was too crowded, and if you came any earlier in the week the shelves were half empty. Norah and Adam came into the town on the first Thursday of their second winter at Inverclachan, and, falling into the habits of the previous year, went their separate ways: Norah to the post office and the vegetable shop; Adam to the butcher's and the chemist's, until they met up in the Co-op.

He had struck up a line of chat with Mr Cheviot, the butcher, the year before, and he was greeted like an old friend. The Parnells ate hardly any meat in England, but here the meat was off the hills and tasted better, and so they ate it regularly. As part of their general briefing in the gossip they had missed while they had been away, Lucinda Goodlands had told them that Mr Cheviot had just been on holiday for the first time in his life, to Bangkok and Manila. So the first thing that Adam said that Thursday in the butcher's was, 'Good morning, Mr Cheviot. And how did you like Bangkok and Manila?' He said it expecting the normal, overawed response of a first-time traveller, and if you were to tell the truth, with a certain amount of condescension, so it was something of a surprise when Mr Cheviot replied in his over-confident way, 'I liked Manila well enough, but Bangkok was a wee bit tame for me.'

Adam could think of nothing to say to this, but stood on his side of the counter looking down at Mr Cheviot and his high-pitched voice.

'Ay,' the butcher went on. 'Mind you, the women were cheaper in Bangkok. You could get any kind you wanted for the price of a cup of coffee.'

Adam was transfixed by his packet of bacon, which Mr Cheviot was wrapping very slowly. He tried putting a fiver on the counter to speed things up a bit. Just then another customer came in and he thought he was saved. It was a pensioner in for her weekly ration of square sausage, but instead of finishing with Adam and serving her himself, Mr Cheviot called someone out from the back of the shop to deal with her. He continued his traveller's tales, changing the content to suit the circumstances.

'Ay, and it was interesting to see what they sold in the butcher shops out there. Nothing like here at all.' His dissertation on the Far Eastern meat trade lasted until the other customer had gone, and then, without a hitch in tone or cadence, he picked up the other subject where he had left off. 'And of course, as I was saying, you never needed to pay more than the price of a cup of coffee for a woman.'

'Don't you think it might be safer to have the cup of coffee,' Adam said, 'these days?'

'Oh no,' Mr Cheviot said, still hanging on to the packet of bacon. 'Is it Aids you're worried about? I looked into all that very carefully. Your chances of getting it from a prostitute in Bangkok are about one in four hundred, and one in a thousand in Manila. So you'd be safe enough.'

Adam said, 'I think I might still prefer the cup of coffee.'

'Oh, you'd be all right,' Mr Cheviot said, 'they cater for all tastes.'

More customers came into the shop, and the butcher rummaged in his pockets and produced small polythene packages, with lockets and chains and bracelets in them, saying exactly how much each had cost in both currencies and how much more they would have cost in Glasgow, and assuring Adam that they were all solid gold. It was another fifteen minutes before Adam could escape with his packet of meat.

He dropped the meat in the car, which was parked by the sea wall, and recrossed the street to the tobacconist's, to get some writing paper. As he was about to enter, the tobacconist's door opened and someone familiar came out.

'Dougie,' he said.

Dougie nodded at him, and said, 'Hello, I heard you were back.'

They stood for a few moments saying small things. Adam was trying to remember if Lucinda had told him anything about the Millars. He remembered that Jean had been pregnant when they left in January and should have had the baby by now, but no one at Inverclachan had mentioned it.

'Has Jean had her baby yet?' he said. He watched Dougie's face as something crossed it: like a smoker when he is caught in the eye with the smoke from his own cigarette.

'Ay,' Dougie said, 'she had a wee girl. The baby died.'

The muscles of Adam's face had been primed for congratulation, and so there was an awkwardness in the expression of pain that crossed his features from one side to the other. He thought about saying that he was sorry, but found that he couldn't see what that had to do with it. 'Is Jean all right?' he said.

'She's fine, healthwise. But you can imagine it's a bit rough. She's better now.' Dougie seemed very calm about it.

'Yes,' Adam said. He thought about asking Dougie how he was himself, but then he thought there was only so much you could ask in a tobacconist's doorway in the rain. He said, 'I know about that death stuff. It's a bit grim. I'll be seeing you, won't I? You'll come down for a drink?'

Dougie said he would. He said that it would be nice. There was something about the way that Adam had dealt with the situation that made him think he could trust the man. They went their separate ways. Adam, once he was inside the shop, had to stop for a minute with his face screwed up in embarrassment. He felt in retrospect that he had been tactless and hurt the man's feelings. The two girls behind the counter set to rearranging chocolate bars so that he wouldn't think that they were watching him. They were used to foreigners behaving oddly: it was best not to take any notice.

Dougie crossed the road feeling lighter. If he had been hurt by the exchange, that was to do with events and nothing to do with what Adam had said. Up until now, everyone he had met knew about the tragedy already, and he hadn't had to say straight out that Kerry was dead. An artificial barrier had been broken, and he went away feeling that he wanted to tell a few more people that his daughter was dead; bluntly; out loud. The pain of it brought him closer to life than he had been since she was born.

When the Parnells had finished all their shopping, and they were driving home across the isthmus towards the clear sky over Inverclachan, Adam told Norah about Mr Cheviot and the cup of coffee, and then, while she was still laughing, he said, 'Did you know that Jean had her baby and it died?'

The tone of his voice stopped Norah sniggering and peeling satsumas. 'No,' she said. 'Oh no.'

He watched her reactions. Perhaps he was being too critical when he thought that they were wrong. He hadn't been happy with his own reactions when he spoke to Dougie. The way she was behaving was normal; it was compassionate; but always at these times he found something missing in her. It seemed to him that he was watching someone who knew the forms of sympathy but had no idea how to feel. She could cry more easily than he, because she knew when crying was called for. With him it was more difficult; he thought that he usually felt things too strongly for crying, for sociable grief.

He felt as he was thinking this that he was being unfair to her; that this was no light in which to be viewing the woman he was supposed to be in love with; but it was in him to make these observations, just as it was in him to walk three paces behind her sometimes, and watch the movement of her shoulders as she walked, out of admiration.

'How did you find out?' she said.

'I met Dougie.'

'What happened?'

'I don't know. I only saw him for a moment. It is odd the Goodlands never told us about it.'

'They have troubles of their own, I suppose.'

'I'm not going into that butcher's again,' he said. 'You will have to get the meat.'

'Me?' she said. 'It's going to be worse for me.'

'It was changing-room talk,' he said. 'You'll be safe from it. Perhaps we should become vegetarian. I don't like the idea of eating flesh that has been through his hands now.'

The next week it was Norah who went into the butcher's, and she came out giggling because she said that Mr Cheviot had been massaging the chicken breasts while talking to her. The final straw was when he asked her, a couple of weeks later, if she liked a read, and gave her a carrier bag full of semi-pornographic novels set in the Far East. Neither she nor Adam would go near the butcher's for the rest of that winter, and in the end they sent the books back with one of the neighbours.

The windows of Joshua's cottage were in need of repair, and rain had been pouring through them in the big storms. About three weeks after the conversation in the tobacconist's doorway Dougie Millar came up from the shore with putty and nails to mend them. It was a bright afternoon with some heat in the sun, and Adam sat out by him to talk while he worked.

As the light began to fade, Norah brought cocoa out to them, and they sat on the window ledges and drank it in the dusk. When Norah had finished hers she walked away and began to move about between the trees. Adam said to Dougie, 'How did you find this place?' Adam was watching Norah closely, fascinated by the way she moved, her shoulders held at an angle that was almost awkward, her hips gliding on a level plane. He thought that he loved her most when she was in motion, even if it was only while he watched her hands when she made cuttings at the bench; there was something in her movement that fascinated him. When Dougie answered his question after a lapse of seconds he had to think back and try to remember what the question was.

Dougie said, 'I lived here as a child, until I was six.'

Adam said, 'What happened then?' Norah had found something among the trees. She was bent over, scrabbling in the moss, and Adam thought that there was something perfect in the moment, and he would have liked to pack the car there and then and go back to Herefordshire, to keep the perfection. He felt just then that anything they had come to Inverclachan for had been achieved, and he couldn't see what would be left to occupy him for the rest of the winter.

Dougie answered again, 'My mother got married.'

'What happened to your father?' Adam said. Norah was walking towards them now, with something in her hands, inspecting it as she walked.

Dougie answered, 'My father and mother weren't married. My father killed himself when I was three.'

Before Adam had to think of something to say to that, Norah had come up to them. She said, 'I think they are chanterelles.' There was a deep-yellow colour glowing in her hands.

Adam said, 'Do you think they might be?' There was greed in his voice. And then he said to Dougie, 'Will you come in for a dram?'

Dougie said that he wouldn't say no.

Adam and Dougie sat at the kitchen table with the whisky bottle between them, while Norah moved around the kitchen with her glass in her hand, cooking the chanterelles. Adam watched her put a fork that was dripping with cream between her lips, and then he remembered that he should be talking to Dougie, who had been silent since he came in. Adam said, 'How did your father kill himself?'

Dougie said, 'He hung himself from a beam in my grandmother's house. I used to stay in the room where he did it, as a child.'

Norah stopped cooking and looked across at them. Her face was bunched up with the appropriate expression. 'Oh dear,' she said. 'How awful.'

'Ay, it was,' Dougie said.

'And why didn't he marry your mother? Was he married already?' Adam asked the question in a deliberately abrupt way to cut across the possibility of sentiment. Norah returned her attention to the chanterelles.

Dougie said, 'She wouldn't marry him. I think that was one of the reasons he killed himself.'

Adam said, 'Perhaps she could see that he was the sort of person who committed suicide.'

Dougie dismissed that idea with a shrug that allowed no possibility of it being viable. And then he said, 'You should see the man she did marry. No one could have been worse than that.' There was a change in the tone of his voice, and Adam realised that the man was about to unburden himself. He felt a slight surge of panic, and tried to think of a trite subject he could change the conversation to, but Norah began speaking.

She said, 'It can't be easy bringing up children.'

Adam couldn't see the relevance of the remark and so could think of nothing to say. Dougie only said, 'Ay,' and seemed upset by it. The light had faded completely outside, and the lighting in the kitchen was bad, and perhaps that allowed him to feel invisible, and more inclined to talk, because when Norah said, 'I'm very sorry about the baby. I've been meaning to go and see Jean,' he began to shake with emotion and talk about the funeral. He was sitting with his back to Norah, and Adam could see both his face and Norah's.

Adam felt awkward and wanted the whole thing to be over quickly; for this man and his sadness to go away, and at the same time he felt it was his duty to sit and listen. It took him some minutes to realise that it wasn't Dougie talking that made him uncomfortable, but the presence of Norah, saying the right things in the right tone of voice, as a sort of punctuation in his speech. He felt that her social conventions were intruding on the privacy of Dougie's grief; it was wrong for him to be talking, to be so upset in these circumstances. He wanted to tell Dougie to be quiet, because he was saying things in a way that Adam himself would not have said them in front of Norah. But he realised, too, that Dougie was not talking because he wanted to talk, but because his silence had crumbled away.

Now Dougie had stopped. He was holding his hands out before him as though they had a small coffin between them, and tears were falling towards where the lid would have been. He seemed unaware that there was anyone else in the room; only gazing at the space between his hands and crying into it.

Adam looked towards Norah. She was crying too, and he found himself cross with her for it. He wanted to tell her to shut up; that this was real and not something she could shanghai to serve her own sentimentality. He felt that the ease with which she produced her tears belittled the profundity of Dougie's. Adam wanted to leave the room, but there was something about Dougie that wouldn't let him. He decided afterwards that it had been a sort of solidarity.

Now both Norah and Dougie were looking at him. Norah's face had swollen with tears, but Dougie's was the same hard angular construction that it had always been: water had flowed from eyes that were naturally miserable over a face that was determinedly inscrutable: there was something hungry for pity about him. Behind him, in Norah's face, he could see a request for a conspirator in her readiness to pity him. Any emotion that Adam could have felt was paralysed by the incompatibility of the two faces before him. He did the only thing he could, which was to look at Dougie and smile, and offer him another dram.

Later, when he was showing Dougie out, he said on impulse, 'What are you doing this Sunday? We could do a long walk. We could bring whisky and drink it at Glen Dubh. I need an excuse for a really long walk.'

Dougie Millar smiled and said, 'Sounds the business.' Adam thought that there was something odd about him as he said it. At the time he didn't realise that he had never seen the man smile before.

When he came back into the kitchen, Norah bit her lower lip and said, 'Oh dear, the poor thing.'

He said, 'Rough, isn't it?' wanting to leave it at that. Now that Dougie was gone his irritation with Norah seemed unreasonable, and he wanted to return to the way he had felt earlier in the evening, when he had been watching her move around, and thinking that he was in love with her.

But she said, 'Perhaps it is as well that we don't have children. I wouldn't want to go through all that.'

And he said, 'That wasn't how it seemed to me.' He regretted the remark once he had made it, and luckily she didn't pursue it. To divert her he said, 'Dougie and I are going for a long walk on Sunday.'

'Oh good,' she said. 'I think he needs someone to talk to. I should visit Jean. What was all that about Dougie's father?'

Adam said, 'He killed himself when Dougie was three. I suppose if you have that sort of background things must be even rougher.' He shocked himself with the tone in which he had said that, and so he added, 'Maybe,' but Norah had bunched her face up again and was saying oh dear. Adam wondered how he had lived with her for so long.

Later, in bed, she said, 'It would be nice if Dougie became your friend. You don't have any real friends.'

'No,' he said, 'I don't.'

She said, 'You beast. You were supposed to say that I was your friend.' She was laughing, the way she often did at his put-downs.

'Sorry,' he said. And after a silence, 'Can people who are married be friends?'

She said, 'I thought so. I thought we were friends.'

'Are we? So why aren't you honest with me?'

'What do you mean?'

'I mean,' he said, 'that in a marriage you have to consider the feelings of the other person because they affect the quality of your life. You have to think about the repercussions of what you will say. That precludes honesty, which is surely the basis of a friendship.'

She said, 'What are you saying?'

'I don't know,' he said. 'It's late. I'm a bit drunk. I can't be making any sense. Don't mind what I'm saying.'

She said, 'Do you love me?'

That was the question he hated most, because he thought that if he did love her she shouldn't need to ask, and if he didn't then it would be more tactful if she never mentioned it. He thought about it, and thought that if there was such a thing in existence as love, then he must love her.

'Of course,' he said. 'What do you think I am doing with you?'

She said, 'Well, that's all right then,' and attached herself to the side of his body. She exuded contentment when she was wrapped around him, and he wouldn't have been able to bring himself to dislodge her.

Someone who liked to look at the sea had once built a wall with a window in it across the mouth of the big cave at Glen Dubh. Inside, there was room for the troglodyte to stand up and walk about, and a stove and cupboards filled with oatcakes and jam. There were chairs on either side of a table by the window, for gazing out at the sea, or playing cards in a fog. At the back of the cave there were even some damp bunk-beds if you felt inclined to stay the night. Mostly these days it was used by Paul Goodlands as a quiet place in which to indulge his wee habit. There was a stash of dope wrapped in oilcloth beneath one of the floorboards.

It was the middle of the afternoon when Adam and Dougie reached the cave on Sunday; a wet blowy day. Dougie and Jean had relations staying and so Dougie couldn't get away until after lunch, and he appeared before Adam looking as though he were setting out on a polar expedition. He wore a balaclava and carried a knapsack. Norah made little jokes about it while Adam put his coat and Wellingtons on, and then she waved them off in a motherly, indulgent way. It wasn't until they were around the bend and going towards the flagpole that they began to feel like men again.

Adam rushed about like a dog, poking at small plants between the rocks, while Dougie walked steadily into the rain, treating the weather as though it was a burden to be shouldered. Adam said, 'It's no good. I've been scanning my mind for deeply sad things to tell you about. For things that might upset me enough to make me burst into tears before you, so that we can be even. I thought things should be evened up. But I can't think of anything. I am a victim of middle-class normality.'

Dougie said, 'That sounds sad enough to me.'

Adam said, 'I know, but it won't make me cry. Look, bog myrtle: if you crush the twigs they smell of soap. When I was a child I used to fantasise about being someone like you. I was always convinced that I was really illegitimate, until I grew up and everyone said how much I looked like my father. I was cycling past two old women one of the days, and I heard one say to the other, "Who's that young fella on the bike?" and the other one said, "I don't know but he's the image of Christian Parnell." And that was that. Sixteen years of illusion shattered. I suppose I had romantic notions about illegitimacy. So what makes you such a sensitive creature? Why aren't you a hooligan out on the terraces?'

Dougie ignored the provocation in his voice, and said, with some gentleness, 'Oh, I've been there, done that.'

When they got to the cave, Dougie unloaded his knapsack, which was full of coffee and lemons and anything else they might need. He lit a gas burner that he had brought with him and boiled some water.

Adam said, 'I've never done this before: syphoned myself off to talk to someone I hardly know. Well, maybe I have, but in my youth. It's making me a bit skittish. You will have to tell me some more sobering facts about your life to quieten me down. I can come on strong with the educated condescending kindness bit and make you feel privileged to have told your troubles to me.'

Dougie said, 'I don't know that there is much to tell.'

Adam said, 'You aren't trying. Things that seem mundane to you are thrilling to people like me, who haven't seen anything of the darker side of life. Were you ever in prison?'

'Only the once,' Dougie said. 'The night before I was married.'

'You see? I told you.' Adam took up the cards and dealt a hand of patience while he talked. 'Do you know this one? My grandmother calls it Eegit's Delight, because it never comes out for her. I find it comes out for me. Were you always the silent type, or was that something you acquired?'

Dougie said, 'I think it was something I learned to do, living with my mother.'

Adam said, 'You aren't afraid of people thinking that you are stupid? Most people – no, I don't mean that, I mean myself. I talk too much, hoping that people will think I am more intelligent than

75

I am. It must take a lot of courage to risk having people think you are a bozo.'

Dougie said, 'It makes life a lot easier.'

Adam said, 'So, tell me about your childhood.'

Dougie said, 'I think I'll need to have a few more drinks before I get into that.'

Adam pushed the bottle across the table and said, 'Work away.' For a few minutes there was only the sound of cards slapping on the table and rain billowing on the window, and Dougie sucking in the smoke of his cigarette. Then Adam said, 'It must be like this going to a prostitute. You know, doing something that is normally an intimate part of an intimate life with someone you hardly know; you wouldn't know enough to trust. Separating off one human activity as if it could be dealt with on its own. That must make a psychiatrist a sort of verbal prostitute; the more so as he's paid for it. Now will you tell me about your childhood?'

Dougie said, 'How much do you want to know?'

Adam said, 'It isn't what I want to know. Want doesn't come into it unless it is how much you want to tell me. For all you know about me I am only keeping the conversation going, out of politeness. Or for all you know, I am here to prove to myself how open-minded I am.'

Dougie said, 'I don't think you are like that.' His voice was serious now, and he was looking at Adam directly.

'So begin at the beginning,' Adam said. 'What were you doing at the moment your father topped himself?'

Dougie said, 'At the moment my father was swinging from a beam in Alexandria, with the insides of his legs soaked in his own urine, I was a wee boy here, living in the big house and playing with mounds of toys as if I was no worse off than anyone else. I wasn't told about my father's death until three years later. I always thought he was alive, and one of the days he was going to come and take me away from Annie Millar.'

'If you really want to tell me about it, start at the start. That's too fast,' Adam said. 'Three years in three sentences is too fast. So, what were you like when you were three years old?'

There was something of kill or cure in what Adam was saying. He wanted to see whether Dougie really needed to talk, and he thought that by irritating him he would give the man his chance to shut up if he wanted. But Dougie was away. He fixed his line of sight somewhere out on the grey sea, and continued.

'Fat. Annie used to overfeed me so that I was a big tumshie with a fat discontented face. My hair was white and curly. I could have been used to advertise Pear's Soap. I suppose I was an unattractive child. I had too much material indulgence from Annie, and not enough love. No love at all. People used to tell her that she was spoiling me, and I don't think that other children liked me. They were jealous of all the toys, and I didn't know how to talk to them. Not that I was often in the company of children my own age. There was Craig Anderson: he wasn't much older than me, and a boy called Alan MacDonald, whose father was the shepherd here, but I never saw much of them. Most of the time I had the run of this place to myself. The Goodlands boys would only be here in their holidays from English school, and not always then. They were a lot older than me, and when they noticed me at all it was to use me as a sort of mascot. Joshua was kind enough to me, and he became my hero. It's funny I used to totter round after him, looking up at him, and now when I see him he only comes up to my armpit and he has to look up to talk to me. Paul used to torture me. He was always tying me to trees and leaving me there for the day. He hasn't changed much over the years.

'I used to follow them all around and let them play with me. Children have a strange sense of their own importance. One day old Mr Goodlands said that he would take his sons for a walk along the shore. Have you heard much about old Mr Goodlands? He was a strange man. It was him who fitted up the cave. And he built the road out the back so that he could drive out here in his Landrover when he was too old to walk. Well, anyway, I followed him out along the shore with Joshua and Paul, and after a while he saw me, and he turned and said, "Go home. I said my sons. You are not one of my sons."

'I was confused by that, even if he was only pointing out the facts, because my mother treated Joshua and Paul as if they were sons of hers. Better than that. She treated them as if they were wee gods, while she was always a bitch with me. She used to have them in her room in the evenings, telling them stories and playing her Elvis records to them. She had a thing about Elvis Presley. Someone told me once that she went out with my father because she thought he looked like Elvis. Not that he did, but he was just as handsome. I used to think that she was disappointed with me because she had conceived me thinking I would be a wee Elvis, and I was a blond curly child. I think my hair went straight and dark later on just to vex her.

'I couldn't understand why I had to be put to bed on summer evenings while the other boys were having a good time with my mother next door. I could hear the music and the laughing, and they knew with the noise they were making that I couldn't be sleeping. Maybe I was younger than them, but it was supposed to be *my* mother, and I had no such considerations from their mother in return. Sometimes when she was putting me to bed, I would ask her if she would tell me a story, and she would say that she didn't know any. At the same time the Goodlands boys were always repeating stories that they said they had heard from my mother. She's a strange woman. You'd have to meet her to know what I'm talking about. But she's dying now. Nearly time she did.

'I used to threaten her with the return of my father. I used to say that my daddy would give me stories when he got back, and she'd be for it then. I said he was going to smash all her Elvis records and take me away with him. I had no memory of him, only a photograph of a man in Highland uniform, and I had made a conquering hero out of him. Whenever I had a dispute with Annie I brought him into it as my only ally. She let me blether on like that for years without telling me he was dead. Sometimes she'd say, "Your father. I'll give you your father. Where is he to look after you?"

'It was my mother who taught me the benefits of stupidity and silence. It wasn't only that she was always telling me how thick I was, but in smaller ways she denigrated everything I did, and belittled me in front of other people, but in a kind of subtle way that suggested to anyone present that she had spoiled and over-indulged me, and given herself nothing but trouble by doing it. I think she tried to convince me that I was stupid because she wasn't that intelligent herself, and she resented the fact that I could argue with her, or that I was better than she was. I had an enquiring mind and she did her best to smother it, and so I adopted a semblance of stupidity as a defensive measure. I was clever enough to work out the advantages of a vacant stare, and the long-term advantages of not saying whatever was on my mind. By the time I was six I was an artist at it. But behaviour becomes a habit, and in the end it takes you over. By the time I was sixteen there was little more than a vacant stare left in me.

'After we had moved away from here, I remembered this place as

78

a sort of paradise on earth. It was, compared to where we moved to. Sort of Eden before the Fall. While I was here there was still hope for me, and a knight in shining fatherhood over the brow of the hill. And it was a world that my mother didn't control. The Goodlands were in charge of our lives, and that was to my advantage. It wasn't that I had allies against my mother, but there were enough other things going on to confuse the issues and save me from her.

'There was a room in the big house. Do you know, if you go down the passage in the west wing, where the estate offices are? There's a small room at the back with no windows. There isn't anything in it now, only old files and junk, but in my day it was used to store things that might be used as presents. I used to spend most of my time in there when the weather was wet. There were new train sets still in their boxes that I used to unpack and play with, and then put back again so that they looked unopened. And piles of books. I must have taught myself to read, because I was reading books in there before I was ever sent to school. And adult presents too. Glasses and china. One year there was a wooden horse in there, and I sat on him for days.

'At Christmas Joshua and Paul would be unwrapping their new train sets, and lording it over me with what Father Christmas had brought them, but I knew better. I never said anything to them, but I enjoyed knowing something that they didn't.

'I realise now that when people spoke of me as a spoiled child they were speaking of me as the housekeeper's son. What they really meant was that I had ideas above my station. With a woman like Annie Millar as the only role model I had of my own class, who could blame me for identifying with the Goodlands?

'When I was six, my mother produced a man called Jimmy Campbell. How or where she found him is a mystery, and how she thought that he could do anything for the quality of her life. It would have been obvious to anyone that he was no good. If you needed proof that my mother was stupid or mad, then you would only have needed to meet Jimmy Campbell. He was a filthy man who drank too much. It might seem unreasonable to mention it, but he had long hairs around his Adam's apple where he couldn't be bothered to shave the whole way down his neck. His fingernails were always dirty. And it wasn't as though he worked manually. He was a part-time security guard, with a lot of braid on his shoulders, and he wore his uniform whenever he could, as if being a part-time security guard was something to be proud of. On other days he used to wear a string vest about the place, and there was hair across the back of his shoulders. He had nothing to offer. He lived on the top floor of a Glasgow tenement with three daughters to look after and no woman. He was looking for someone to keep house for him, and to push the responsibility of minding his daughters on to. I suppose that my mother could have been looking for a man to push the responsibility of looking after me on to. This man, a complete stranger, and disgusting to boot, was presented to me as my new father, and I was supposed to start calling him Dad, straightaway, even before the wedding.

'If it was only that my mother had had her fill of Inverclachan; had had enough of scenery and service, she could have looked around her and done better for herself. I always thought that she married Jimmy Campbell to punish me and bring me down a peg, because living with the Goodlands had given me expectations of life that I had no right to have in her eyes. I used to look at the photograph I had of my father and decide that I was going to be just like him. Already I was stretching out of my fatness to be a big gaunt child, and my eyes were sinking back in my head the way his did. As I grew to be more like my father, she hated me more, and chose the man who was least like Iain MacLeod in order to hurt me. A small, rum-stained, hideous man.

'Faced with this marriage, I abandoned my silence and objected to it. I raised my father in all his phantom glory and became quite articulate for someone my age. She had nothing in the way of argument that she could use against me, and so she used the weapon that she had been saving. She said, "You are getting far too big for your boots, boy, but I'll sort you."

'We were in the kitchen of the big house. I was standing by the long table, holding on to it because my knees were shaking. My two kneecaps were going up and down like pistons, but out of rhythm with each other. I was trying to contain the shaking to parts of my body that were hidden by the table so that she wouldn't know. She was mixing something at the range. She moved away from it slowly and wiped the flour from her hands with a towel. By this time she was hugely fat and had high blood-pressure. She used to wheeze as she moved around the house. She told me to stay where I was and she went away up the back stairs.

'I had no idea what was in store for me, and so I sat on a chair and waited. I spent the time thinking of cruel things to say to her, and trying to work out how I could contact my father and get taken away with him. I knew I had a granny somewhere because I got Christmas and birthday cards from her. I thought that her address must be in my mother's handbag somewhere and I decided that I would go to her room as soon as I could and look through it. There would be no danger of being caught. You could hear my mother clumping and wheezing towards you a mile off.

'When she came back she was holding the handbag that I had been thinking about. She rested it and her elbows on the dresser while she got her breath back, and then slowly, and while still panting, she opened it and began to look through it. I thought for a moment that she was going to give me my grandmother's address and be rid of me. But she took out a newspaper cutting and unfolded it. Then she searched for her glasses and read it.

'She said, "If you're so good at reading, see if you can read this," and she held it out to me. I wouldn't get out of my chair because I thought that my knees would start to shake again and I didn't want her to see it happen. So she had to cross the kitchen and hand it to me herself.

'The cutting was three years old. The date had been written across the top of it in Biro, and beneath it the headline said ALEXANDRIA SUICIDE. I read how Iain MacLeod had hung himself from a beam and how the door had to be broken down, and he was mourned by his mother and sisters, and it even gave my grandmother's address. In the middle of it all the only thing I could grasp was that address.

'I don't know what my mother's expression was, because I couldn't look at her. She shuffled back to the range and whatever she was baking. I went out of the kitchen and down to the shore.

'They came looking for me with torches after dark, and it took them a long time to find me. I wasn't hiding or anything, only sitting between some rocks and not answering them. I thought that if I sat there long enough I would die like my father. If heroes committed suicide, then that was the thing for me. At the time I hadn't started to be angry with my father for killing himself. That came later.

'Annie's little revelation kept me quiet long enough for her to marry Jimmy Campbell. It kept me quiet longer than that. When I trace things back, it always seems that the trouble started that day; that everything since is a direct consequence of that day. Even Kerry. Kerry could never have died if my mother hadn't set out to destroy me that day in the kitchen.'

'The biggest shock of moving to Glasgow was maybe the language barrier. I had no idea what anyone was saying to me, and after living in the big house for all those years I talked like a fucking wee Etonian myself. I even used Etonian slang, without being aware of it. Whenever I opened my mouth in the street a fist would land in it. It took me a while to work out why, because as far as I was concerned I talked normally. It was only a constantly bruised gob that made me learn the patter, but even after that I was seen to be different enough to bear the brunt of quite a bit of violence. "Stitch this" was the first Glasgow phrase I became thoroughly acquainted with. The most useful tactics I had to avoid being beaten up were blank stares and silence.

'We were living in a tenement in the Maryhill Road. A lot of them are pulled down now, but if you go down there you can still see a few of the buildings. We had the top flat, and, because Annie had got so fat, she couldn't manage the stairs and became a sort of prisoner. But she was always polishing the front doorstep in case anyone came to see her; and she kept a best sitting-room for visitors that no one was allowed to go into. Not that she ever had any visitors. She had, maybe, come off her hinges a little. She hated me.

'I had to change my name to Campbell along with my mother. But if anyone asked me who I was I still told them I was Dougie Millar. Maybe that was one of the reasons I didn't get along so well at school, since I couldn't identify with the person they were calling Campbell. When they called out Dougie Campbell in class I used to look around me to see who was meant. After I got used to them meaning me I saw no reason to change my attitude.

'Annie had some more children for Jimmy Campbell. It was bad news for me because until then I was the only boy and had a room to myself, but after Humie came along I had to share with him. They were supposed to be my brothers and sisters, but as far as I was concerned they were nothing to do with me. My only blood-tie to them was through my mother and I couldn't see that that counted for anything. The strange thing about Annie was that she seemed to hate these other children as well. Since she didn't have to be nice in front of the Goodlands any more it seemed there was nothing but spite and bitterness left in her. Why did she go on bringing children into the world when she was only going to fuck them up with her hatred? That's a sore one. Whenever she had enough of us older ones we were packed off into council homes while she had a wee holiday.

'I knew about these homes already because I had a friend called Ben who had been in one himself. Ben was the only friend I had at the time, because he was black and no one would talk to either of us. I've heard people say that there was never racism in Scotland, but I can only think that those people have never been down the Maryhill Road. Ben had a worse time than I ever did, but while I could change my accent or shut up, there was nothing he could do about his colour.

'They set up a fight in the school between Ben and me. It was the bottom of the heap against the next one up. They were all on my side because at least I was Scottish, and the object of the exercise was to prove that even the worst of us was better than any black. No one had taken into consideration that Ben was smaller than me and even more demoralised. Have you ever been in a fight? I don't know what happens, myself, but once you are in a fight, you fight. It has maybe something to do with anger. Once you're there you just want to smash the other guy up. I had wee Ben pinned to the ground, and I was about to do him in; but he wasn't fighting back any more. He was just looking at me. And then I looked up and there was this circle of red faces screaming at me to finish him off. They were hysterical. Giving detailed instructions to me about what to do next.

'The surrealism of trying to decide which piece of advice to take kind of evaporated any anger I had, and then I couldn't remember why I was fighting in the first place. I just stood up and walked away, and Ben walked after me. They were all shouting after us, and throwing stones. I remember a stone hitting me in the shoulder. After that, Ben hung around me until he made himself my friend. We were supposed to look out for each other, but the reality was that we got done-in together. Then one time Ben disappeared for about three months and when he got back he told me about the home.

'Things were getting rough in the Maryhill Road. Humie was about a year and a half old and Annie was pregnant again. She could hardly move between her weight and the blood-pressure and being pregnant. She and Jimmy seemed to hate each other. His own daughters weren't that well-adjusted either, or that easy to deal with. I had to go and have my appendix out and when I was just out of hospital Jimmy was playing around with me with a chair-leg. I don't know if it was an accident or if he was drunk or what, but the chair-leg went into me and broke the stitches, and I had to go back to hospital. It was horrific. You should see the scar sometime.

'Anyway, it was about that time that we had a Care and Protection Order slammed on us. Me and the three girls. I don't know if Annie was incapable of looking after us, or even if she was, why she put me in the home rather than sending me to stay with my grandmother. That's a sore one. I found out later that my grandmother was always offering to have me, but she wasn't even allowed to see me.

'Being in the home was even worse than living with my mother. That's saying a lot. When I woke up in the morning my bed would be covered in boots, because the other boys in the dormitory said that I shouted in my sleep, and they threw the boots to shut me up. Talk about survival. I could deal with any wee bastard when I came out of that place. But it isn't as simple as that. Do you know what happens to a child when you put him in an institution? He loses his power. You get to thinking that you have no control over any of the events in your life. Once you do that you're a prisoner for ever. You only have to look at the English and the public-school system. You get people who are willing to perpetuate the system.

'I don't want to talk about that place any more. That place is still in me. But being there had one beneficial effect. It broke any dependency I had on my mother and the Maryhill Road. I knew that I was out on my own and I couldn't depend on anyone else to look after me. I had nothing of value to lose. As soon as we were sent back to Annie, after she had her child, I ran away from home, to my grandmother in Alexandria.

'I already had my grandmother's address from the newspaper clipping, and I stole some money. I was fairly good at stealing by now. I knew my way round most of the shops in the Great Western Road, but to steal money I had to go through my mother's handbag. I also stole the only suitcase we had from the top of the wardrobe. The suitcase was nearly as big as myself, and the clothes I had just about lined the bottom. But I wasn't going to turn up at my grandmother's carrying a paper parcel, like a tramp.

'Of course she was delighted to see me. Of course. What can I say about her? And of course I was brought back to the Maryhill Road. Several times. They even tried sending me back to the home for a spell to sort me out. But I just kept running away to Alexandria until they let me stay there.

'After that I had what you might call a normal childhood. My grandmother lived in the house over the tobacconist's with my Auntie Mary. When I moved in Auntie Mary gave up her bedroom in the front for me and shifted into the back one with my grandmother. My grandmother used to talk to me. She was always telling me how handsome and clever I was and how I was just like my father. She asked me once why I never smiled. She said my father had a good smile.

'Religion was a bit of a problem for them. They were Catholic, but they knew my mother was Presbyterian. My granny didn't think it would be right if I started in on Catholicism, or maybe she thought that she might get into trouble over it and lose me. At the same time she thought it might be stretching the possibility of my salvation a bit if she sent me to the Wee Frees. So she used to send me to the Baptists for Sunday school to get my bit of God. That was what she used to say. She used to brush my hair on Sunday and send me off to get my bit of God. And then she would go to the hallstand and open a drawer that was only opened on Sunday and get out her missal and her black gloves. I used to wait to watch her put the gloves on, because they were so wee I never thought that they would fit. But they used to slide over her hands; over the liver-spots and the arthritic knuckles and make her hands look as fine as anyone's. She wore the same gloves for Mass in the summer and winter. I got to think those gloves were holy or something. Then she would shake holy water on me as we were going out the door, and she would turn right with Mary, and I would turn left on my own.

'The years in Alexandria were good. They were nearly normal. There were the usual bad things too. There was a strange old uncle who used to take me and my cousins to the cinema and give us sweeties if we did unspeakable things to him. But that is no more than most children have to go through. Even if we were being exploited at least it was a contract we entered of our own free will. My cousins were fairly horrible too; but those things are easily forgotten. They must be easily forgotten or none of us would be sane. An isolated sexual event which is kept secret is something that anyone could cope with, if it involves strangers and your own decision. Something that your mother is complicit in is another thing.

'My grandmother died when I was fifteen and that was the end of Alexandria. By that time my mother and Jimmy Campbell had moved to Fort William, and that was the only place I had to go.'

The afternoon had faded out, and hard rain had come on, driving towards the window they were sitting by. Dougie's voice had lost its gutturalism and become soft and continuous, like a Highlander's voice. The cave faced west, and the coast of Jura had been fading to black. As it disappeared, Adam said, 'I have never been to Jura. I wonder what it is like?'

Dougie said, 'Neither have I.'

Adam said, 'This is all very one-sided. I am sorry to be letting you do all the talking.'

Dougie said, 'So long as you aren't sorry to be doing the listening.'

Adam said, 'No.'

Dougie boiled some more water, and found candles on a shelf above the door, and lit one and put it on the table between them. Then he went outside to pee. Adam thought: I could be fond of this man, I suppose. But he is the one who is looking for a friend. I see no reason why he is telling me these things, unless it has to do with me being as far removed from his childhood as it is possible. There must be some theory of inversions, where to prove a truth you have to measure its opposite against it, and if both are true then you are vindicated. This is whisky thinking. But he is hardly a kindred spirit to me. He says that his mother never loved him and I believe it. There is nothing in him that would suggest a mother's love. His father had the good grace to allow him to grow up without a father's influence, while mine had the bad grace to outlive my mother. Why is this man still so sad? This is a man who has never fallen in love, I think. I wonder what would happen to him if he fell in love?

Dougie came in again, brushing the rain out of his hair. He settled himself on the other side of the candle, and began to make a roll-up.

Adam said, 'You shouldn't smoke, you know. I can never bear the people I am fond of to smoke. My mother died of lung cancer. The first thing I did when I met Norah was to make her give up smoking. But that's no good either. I think that if I left her tomorrow she would light up straight away. She smokes behind pillars at parties.'

Dougie inhaled a vast gulp of the smoke and let it out slowly so that it climbed his face inch by inch, past the mouth with no lips and the tight skin and the miserable eyes. He said, 'I'm sorry.' Adam thought about it for a moment, and then realised that Dougie was apologising for smoking, for hurting Adam's sensibilities.

Dougie said, 'So, you're leaving Norah tomorrow.'

Adam said, 'I said if. You can't take anything for granted. It's no good being with someone because you feel that you have to be. I sometimes think of going away on my own, slowly down through France and Spain and Morocco, and on into the unknown. I know nothing about the countries beyond Morocco. That is deliberate. I avoid information about them so that when I get there I won't know what to expect. And there are islands somewhere, off the coast of Africa, called the Isles Vertes. That is, I think, the end of the journey.'

Dougie said, 'I was thinking myself that Inverclachan would be no bad place to leave Jean and the children behind. They would miss me less here. Not that I think they would miss me at all. But I haven't worked out where to go yet. So far it's only wanting to get away.'

'Been there,' Adam said. 'Done that.'

Dougie smiled again at the sound of Adam imitating him.

'So,' Adam said, 'what happened next?'

Dougie said, 'I went to Corby and got a job in a steelworks.'

Adam said, 'No, you're skipping. What about this sexual betrayal that your mother was complicit in? And how come you got to leave school at fifteen? And who told you that Corby was the place to go?'

Dougie said, 'The devil must be waiting for my mother, now she's nearly dead. I sometimes think about his long fingernails scoring into her flesh. It isn't a wish or a fantasy; it's a projection of reality. So anyway, you want to know about the glorious night I lost my virginity. In Fort William.

'The flat we had there was more crowded than the flat in the Maryhill Road. One of Jimmy's daughters had run off and no more was heard of her. The other two were both pregnant by unnamed persons, and my mother had had four children by Jimmy. Annie still kept the best room and the doorstep, but these days she had a friend who used to visit. An old crow called Morag who used to drop by to talk to her now and again.

'One night Morag had a dram too many and elected to stay the night. She was given the sofa in the best room to sleep on. I had long gone to bed myself, in the wee high-ceilinged room I shared with Humie. The room was the width of the window and the length of two beds, toe-to-toe. The walls were grey and they went up into darkness because the ceiling was navy-blue, and it was like sleeping at the bottom of a well. The whole flat was filled with the horrible animal sounds and smells of sleep. For some reason I had the door locked. I always locked it, and Annie used to scream at me about it because she thought I was masturbating, but she couldn't stop me locking it. It was a bolt that was built into the wood, and not a lock and key.

'In the middle of the night Morag came banging on the door. At first I ignored her, thinking that someone else would wake up and drag her back to her bed, but everyone else in the flat was behaving like corpses. With the noise she was making she must have woken them all, but because she was calling out my name, and because her intentions were fairly plain, everyone else just pretended to be asleep, or maybe they were enjoying the entertainment. The bastards. Even Humie, whose bed was nearer the door than mine was, kept curled up with his eyes shut. He had lived long enough with Annie Campbell to know when to lie doggo. In the end I had to open the door for Morag and let the old bitch in to shut her up.

'She wanted sex with me. I thought that she would never do it because of the child in the next bed, but that didn't seem to bother her, so I said to her, "If you're serious, let's see you get your gob round that then." And she did, and then I fucked her and she went away. So much for a sensitive boy being taught the fine art of love by an understanding older woman. She was horrible. She was ugly and she was old.

'The next day I asked my mother if she had heard all the racket and why the fuck she hadn't done anything about it.

'She shrugged her bulk and revolved her eyes away from me, and while she was looking down into the road she said, "It's only nature."

'Anyway, I was finished with school by that stage. I was finally expelled for setting the toilets on fire, but they could have used plenty of other reasons for getting rid of me. I was never a model student.

'The only thing that happened to me in school of any lasting value was that I met Jean. She was sort of my girlfriend. I don't know why. I looked across the yard and there was this pair of eyes looking back at me. I don't know what was in her eyes, but I've never seen it in anyone else's. Anyway, that was it. She had something in her eyes and here we still are eighteen years later. Is it eighteen years?

'I couldn't stay in Fort William, and there was nothing for me to do there even if I wanted to. Then I had a letter from someone I knew called Kenny Stewart. He was working in the steelworks in Corby and he said he was lonely down there and for me to go and join him, so I did. That was in April '73. How long was I there? I can't remember: I was there the summer, and the winter. That place was so horrible I can hardly remember anything about it. Even then I could see that it would be better to be penniless in Scotland among your friends than have a wage in England. I haven't been back to England since. It's a terrible place. You should know all about that. You have to live there. I wouldn't.

'All the time I was there I used to lie awake at night thinking about Alexandria and the hills and the tough boys of Renton, and even romantic crap like fog on Loch Lomond; and I could always see Jean's eyes in the dark above my bed. I still didn't know what her eyes meant, and so one morning I told everyone to fuck off and I hitch-hiked back to Scotland, and ended up on her doorstep at four o'clock on a February afternoon, and I just stood there dripping until they asked me in. Her house was in the same road as my grandmother's house, and so I suppose it was the closest I could get to home.

'After that I lived with Jean and her parents for a while. It wasn't wonderful but it was the best I could do. It took me until the summer to find a job, and that was as a sawmill operator, in Fort William, of all places. I went up and found a flat, and Jean left school and left her parents to live with me. She got a job working in a hardware shop. Her parents weren't ecstatic or anything. They weren't pushing for a wedding. I think they were hoping that she would grow out of me.

'There was nothing mind-bending about the job. It was driving tractors and fork-trucks and playing with saws. I didn't like it particularly, or living in Fort William, but we were there three years. In the meantime we got married. That was when I had my one night in prison. It was only because I got drunk with some of the boys in Helensburgh the night before and we ripped the place up a bit. We were shut in for the night, but they let us out in the morning in time to change for the wedding. Well, what can I say? This life of mine must be boring you to death. It should. Most of it bored me to death.'

'No, no,' said Adam. 'This is nowhere near my threshold of boredom. You should try a conference on plant marketing. I just love hearing about your sweet little heart-breaking life.'

Neither of them wore a watch, and so it was impossible to tell what the time was. There was only blackness outside the cave, and rain thrown against the window. Several times Adam had thought that they should be heading back, but then he would think that if they waited another few minutes the rain would ease off. But the rain was steady and he was too relaxed with the whisky to suggest that they go out in it. His feet got cold, and he took his boots off and drew them up beneath him. Sitting on his feet cut the circulation off, but that was comfortable and relaxing too in its way. The bottle on the table was two-thirds empty. Dougie took the coffee from his knapsack and began to brew that, to make a change. They finished the rest of the whisky in coffee, and then drank coffee on its own. It was always Dougie who was up and mothering and being the one who made it. Adam knew that his legs were sealed-in beneath him, and that if he moved at all he would be uncomfortable. Dougie went outside to pee every so often.

Adam said, 'You have a terrible weak bladder.'

'Ay,' Dougie said, and then he said, 'it's the coffee.'

Adam said, 'Terrible stuff, coffee. You shouldn't drink it.'

Adam wondered if he was drunk, and decided that he was in a state that was neither one nor the other. He thought how lucky Dougie was to have met such a sympathetic listener, just when he needed to talk so much. And he thought how lucky he was himself to have had such a straightforward middle-class existence; to have had such a relatively normal childhood. Then, while he was still ashamed of his own arrogance, he said, 'I had a friend once, who looked a bit like you. We used to talk all night.'

Dougie said, 'What happend to him?'

'I don't know. He fell away. A sort of moral suicide, I suppose. We both thought that we could do anything we wanted, and he turned out to be incapable of doing anything at all.'

'I had one of those myself,' Dougie said.

Adam said, 'I gave up on friendship after that.'

Dougie began to laugh. It was not a nice laugh; there was something demonic in it, so that his teeth seemed yellow and his eyes evil. Adam wondered if it was the effect of the whisky which made him seem like that, but all the same he was irritated with Dougie for it. He looked about in his mind for a small dagger to stab him with.

'You have never been in love, have you?' he said. 'I know that you have never been in love.'

Dougie stopped laughing, and looked at him seriously.

Adam said, 'I suppose I could make you fall in love with me if I wanted to. I am good at making people fall in love with me. Then what would you do?'

Dougie said, very softly and seriously, 'I hope it won't come to that.'

Adam knew then that they were both drunk. He thought that the best thing to do was probably to resume his silence. He said, 'So whatever brought you back to Inverclachan?'

Dougie wasn't looking at him any more, but at the end of his own cigarette. 'You're skipping now. I was still in Fort William, sitting on a fork-truck. We moved to Rhu in about '76, because I got a job there with the Ministry of Defence. The Royal Corps of Transport, of all things a patrolman. Can you believe it? Responsible for security during the silent hours, and security passes and clearance of workforce and visitors. I was right in there. I was even in the Masons. I found out afterwards that I only got into the Masons because I was using my own name again by that time. There were people who would have objected to Dougie Campbell if his name had come up, but no one knew who Dougie Millar was, and so I got in.

'I was in Rhu for about a year, and then I took my first step into Coulport. I suppose I felt fine about it at the time. It was some sort of career, and I was someone who'd always been told that I would never amount to anything. And I got a lot of reading done. There was a lot of free time in the MOD. I got through two or three books a week. They used to call me Benny Glum there, because people thought I looked so miserable. That was Coulport.

'Until the Falklands War I was settled enough in that job. Maybe I should say the Malvinas War now, so there's no doubt about my sympathies on that one. I was doing fine for myself, getting promoted and passing their wee exams. There was no need for educational qualifications. Whatever they needed you to do they could train you to do it. I used to go on courses for them, but mostly it was a question of knowing when it was a good thing to sign your name in the wee box at the end of a sheet of paper, and knowing when it was better to get some other poor bastard to sign it; I got very well up on the dog-eat-dog system. No bother, pal. Besides, I had no choice. From what I could see the MOD were the only solvent employers left between Paisley and Skye, unless you wanted to step back into the Middle Ages and become a ghillie or a serf or something. All my friends were either working for the Ministry or on the dole. So I just pedalled along, studying the system until I was the man in charge. I wasn't in charge of much, but it was enough to keep me amused. I had a torpedo-inspection team under me. I never thought much about the torpedoes, but I used to get off on giving out orders; on being able to lose my temper with subordinates; and it was a cushy number. There was never that much to do, apart from reading novels. The system was fine with me and I got to be a darling of the Official Secrets Act.

'The time that the *Belgrano* got hit, the people in our department went wild. It seemed that the torpedo that did the job was a Mark 8, which was the one we were working with. It wasn't necessarily one of ours, but they were celebrating the possibility that it might have been. I couldn't believe it. Men were going around with big smiles on their faces and slapping each other on the back. These were supposed to be Scotsmen; celebrating because they had helped the English prime minister to kill a lot of Argentinians and bolster her opinion-poll ratings. I felt sick about it. I'd never even met an Argentinian. Up until then I had been inspecting torpedoes without thinking about them being used, but if I did, I assumed that they were supposed to stop a Russian invasion or something. It was supposed to be the Ministry of *Defence*. I never thought that they'd be used so that three sheep farmers in the middle of the Atlantic could be saved a technical irregularity on their passports. The people I worked with were drunk on their victory, but I was back with the silence and the vacant stares.

'The fact that the ship was headed away from the Falklands at the time it was sunk didn't come out for a while after that. I felt a bit helpless about it. Jean and I were in debt and wee Iain was just a baby, and I didn't think I could just walk away from the job. I became a sort of fifth columnist. I used to tack up newspaper articles about the *Belgrano* in the locker-room. That sort of thing. And I started to take a lot of sick-leave. In '84 I had a hundred and sixteen days sick-leave. That was about the time that I was found talking to some peace campers who were campaigning against Trident. They were set up around the base and I was seen having a cup of coffee with them. When I went back into the depot the MOD police took my pass number and by lunchtime the next day I was a security risk.

'For the next two years I had a sort of battle with them. Without a security pass I was barred from most of the base and so if I did go into work there was nothing to do but sit in the locker-room reading the papers. I had three hundred and twenty-four days sick-leave in '85 and three hundred and sixty-five days in '86. They were trying to get me to resign, but if I resigned without good reason I wouldn't get dole so I said they would have to sack me. They knew that if they sacked me I would go for unfair dismissal and there would be publicity. So I got sick-leave. Then I had to prove that I had been made unfit for work because of the stress that the nature of the job had put on my conscience. I had to prove some sort of mental breakdown, which I suppose was what I had had. I spent a lot of those last two years sitting around with welfare officers and medical officers and MOD psychiatrists, and doing wee tests like you'd give to a white rat, until in the end they couldn't be bothered fucking me around any more and gave me premature retirement on grounds of inefficiency due to unsatisfactory attendance.

'The house we lived in at the time belonged to the Ministry. I couldn't see that there was anything to life in Rhu on the dole. I didn't see us like that. Scraping pennies to hire a video because there was nothing else to look at. All the time I was thinking about Inverclachan. I hadn't been back here for years. When I lived with my granny I used to come back for holidays sometimes, but as I got older it was harder to fit in among the people. By the time I was the sort of delinquent youngster who sets the school on fire there didn't seem to be anything here for me at all.

'I thought if I was going to be on the dole I might as well be collecting it in paradise. I thought about doing other things, but I couldn't. It was a sort of paralysis. When I thought about any of the jobs I could do there was always going to be someone down the line who would suffer as a result of me doing it. There isn't anything in this world you can do without hurting someone somewhere. So I decided to be a contemplative. The world needs more contemplatives. There used to be monasteries all over the place stuffed with them. But these days no one thinks. The people with the leisure to think are all on a high-sugar diet because it's the only thing they can afford, and they just watch soap operas. You can't think if you watch soap operas. That's me. Redressing the balance in the spiritual energy of the world. Or that was the idea. This was supposed to be paradise, and Kerry was supposed to be the child born in paradise. The whole thing seems to have gone a bit wrong. Perhaps being a contemplative isn't the cushy number I thought it might be.'

Adam thought that maybe it was time to go. Dougie was staring at his hands again and the cold had become pervasive. He thought it must be eight or nine o'clock, and Norah would be wondering where he had got to. He said, 'I think we should be getting back. So that was it? You bundled your family into a car and brought them here?'

Dougie looked up from his hands, offended. 'It was a democratic decision. The only vote against was wee Jessica. She didn't want to leave her friends. She still hasn't forgiven me.'

They stumbled down the hill and across the fields and through the woods. Once they were outside the rain seemed less severe. As they got near Adam's house, he said, 'I don't understand something. When you saw Jean's eyes across the playground, was that all there was to it? There must have been more.'

Dougie said, 'What do you think?'

'I think you saw the eyes of someone who was in love with you. That was something you hadn't seen before. Maybe not since.'

Dougie said, 'If you knew that, why did you ask?'

'I wanted to know if you knew it.' And without hesitating, Adam said, 'I told you a lie earlier on. I said that I was always talking so that people didn't think I was stupid. It isn't true. I hardly ever open my mouth normally. I just didn't want you to know the effect you

96

had on me, because I don't understand why you should have that effect. The things I say to you would make me feel naked if I said them to anyone else.'

By that time they were passing the house, and Dougie said good-night and shook Adam's hand and went on towards the shore. Adam went inside wondering why there were no lights on in the house. He thought Norah might be away visiting, but the car was still outside, and she wouldn't have gone on foot in the rain. He went into the kitchen and drank a pint of water and filled a jug to take to bed with him. The stove was cold to the touch and there was no evidence that Norah was in the house. He went down to the bedroom and turned the light on. She was sitting up in bed with her face stained from hours of crying. He thought there must have been a disaster of some kind.

'What's the matter?' he said.

She said, 'It's half-past three in the morning.'

'No,' he said. 'It can't be.' He looked at the clock by the side of the bed and saw that it was, and saw that he couldn't refute it. He began to undress. 'I thought it was still the evening,' he said.

'Where have you been?' she said, and started a fresh flood of tears. She had been happy enough for the afternoon; had become a little melancholic towards evening and gone to bed early. Several sleepless hours alone in bed had produced a quiet steady sobbing, and she was overcome with a sense of foreboding that was no less strong for being irrational. She couldn't imagine what had happened to Adam; had visions of his mangled body at the bottom of a cliff; at other times thought that he was betraying her in some way. She had lived for years with a man who had never left her alone for an evening without an explanation, and the novelty of abandonment induced dramatic thoughts in her head. So when she heard the murmur of men's voices passing the bedroom window, and she should have been relieved that he was returning to her, she felt instead a thread of anger. That could easily have evaporated if she hadn't heard him singing and whistling to himself as he entered the house and fiddled about in the kitchen. There was something careless in his tone that alarmed her. She thought, as she heard it, that it was the singing of a man who had just made a conquest. So when she asked him where he had been, there was an anger and an accusation in her voice which they were both aware of, and it was the sound of her own voice saying it that produced the new tears.

'Talking,' he said, and he began to laugh. He couldn't understand why he was laughing at the time; it was not out of nervousness; it was a genuine free laugh, that might have only been a smile if he hadn't been so aware of the difference between her state of mind and his.

She said, 'You are drunk.'

'No,' he said.

She said, 'I can smell whisky.'

'I had some whisky,' he said. 'I'm not drunk.'

And again she said, 'Where have you been?' This time the anger in her voice was edging towards hysteria.

'Oh, for Christ's sake,' he said, pulling the bedcovers up about him, and settling in with his back to her, 'how many brothels are there within walking distance of Inverclachan?'

'This is it,' she said. 'This is the beginning of the end.'

'Of what?' he said.

She said, 'I am losing you. I can feel it.'

He could think of several answers to that, but he couldn't summon the interest to make any of them. He lay still and waited for her to put her arms about him, and then made love to her in a dazed, half-conscious, sleep-inducing way.

She was silent all the next morning, and went about the house with a martyred expression. By lunch he had had enough of it. He said, 'So what's this supposed to be? A little punishment? Is this supposed to make me beg your forgiveness because I spent a few hours talking to someone else? You were the one who encouraged it. Go and have a friendy-wendy, you said. I didn't see the subclause about being home by ten.'

She said, 'It was half-past three in the morning.'

He said, 'I wasn't wearing a fucking watch. And if I had been I don't see what difference it would have made. That's how long it took. The man told me his life. What was I supposed to say? Oh sorry, Dougie, it's half-eight. My mother-figure at home will be worrying. We can do '76 to '82 next Sunday. Have a nice week?'

She said, 'But you could have been anywhere.'

He said, 'I couldn't.' And then he thought for a moment and said, very quietly, 'In any case, none of this is what's worrying you. Either you should be honest about what you are thinking, or shut up. You want a child so that you can consolidate your possession of me and love the child, and then you wouldn't have to love me any more. It worries you if I talk to someone else, because you want some sort of exclusive right.'

Her only defence was to look at him as if she couldn't understand what he was saying, and then, in an exasperated outburst, to say, 'It isn't only me. I'm sure Jean was out of her mind with worry too,' and with some faintly operatic gestures she pushed her plate away and got up from the table and left the house. He watched her climb the hill at the back while he finished what he was eating. It almost choked him, but he ate it as though he was determined it wouldn't.

And then he did a terrible thing. He put his coat on and found his Wellingtons, and made for Shore Cottage.

As he was knocking on the Millars' door, he thought to himself: I am only doing this to prove that I am right and the woman I am supposed to be in love with is a psychotic loon. Is that something I want to know? But by then he had already knocked, and there was nothing to do but hope that there was no one at home. Jean answered the door.

She was not quite herself yet after Kerry's death. Her complexion was bad and she seemed smaller than Adam had remembered her, despite the fact that her waistline was still slightly bloated from the pregnancy. He found himself examining her eyes carefully to see what it was about them that you could pinpoint across a schoolyard. They were normal, large brown eyes. It must have been love. He repressed an urge to tell her straightaway that she looked as though she could do with some vitamin C, realising that it was the sort of opening remark that Lucinda would have made.

She seemed pleased to see him. She asked him into the house and he followed her. He said, 'I came to apologise to you, really. I kept Dougie out until all hours last night.'

'I had a feeling he'd be gone a while,' she said.

He said, 'We got talking. I hope you didn't wait up.'

'I never heard him come in,' she said. 'But I knew it must have been late. He's only getting up now.'

And he thought: Point proven. It's you who's mad, Norah, not me. And as soon as he had thought that, he found himself wondering about Jean; wondering whether she was a downtrodden wife, and didn't have a mind of her own; whether it was out of passivity that she didn't mind her husband being out all night. But as he was thinking this, he went on talking nonsense, politely. 'We got to drinking coffee. Terrible stuff, coffee.'

Jean said, 'Ay. I thought I could smell coffee on his breath.'

She said it in such a wry, flirtatious way, that he was ashamed of himself for what he had just been thinking about her.

'I was as sick as a dog this morning after it,' he said.

She said, 'I won't offer you any then. Tea?'

'What kind have you got?'

'Tea-bags,' she said. 'I think there might be some of that Earl Grey somewhere.'

He contorted his face as if it was a monumental decision. He said, 'Tea-bags, I think. Earl Grey is only bad tea disguised by bergamot. It's better to take your chances with tea-bags. But as weak as you can make it.'

She said, 'In that case you better make it yourself.'

While he was carefully dipping one corner of his tea-bag into the cup, she said, 'It's good he had someone to talk to.'

'That's the theory,' Adam said. 'What about yourself? It must have been rougher on you.'

'Kerry?' she said.

'Kerry,' he said.

'It's better now,' she said. 'I was bad for a while.'

Adam said, 'It can't be easy.'

She said, 'Usually, when someone dies there are things to remember. When my granny died last year, everyone spent days sitting around and talking about her and all the things she did, and it made it better. But when there's hardly anything to talk about, and you aren't grieving over memories.'

'Grieving over expectations?' he said.

She said, 'In some ways I think it's harder on wee Jessica. She was really looking forward to the baby, and now she keeps telling everyone that her baby sister died. I don't think she understands it.'

Adam said, 'I thought it was supposed to be easier at that age.' Then he added, 'But from talking to Dougie about his childhood, I can see that Jessica might be a bit of an exception.'

She smiled at him, and then became serious again, and said, 'Ay, Kerry's death brought a lot of things back I thought Dougie was over.'

Adam said, 'You never get over those things.' He had the feeling that he had driven that conversation into the ground, so he said, 'Do you miss living in Rhu at all?'

She thought about that for a while, and said, 'I miss bits of it. But it's better here. It's better for the children.'

He was about to tell her that she couldn't have enough to do here, but he was saved by Dougie coming into the room, because he wouldn't have realised until after he had said it how condescending it would have been.

'Hello there,' Dougie said. 'It's Adam the man.'

Adam said, 'You're a bit cheerful. I suppose I would be if I didn't get up until this hour. I have to be up before eight or I can't live with myself. The Protestant work ethic. I must have a Protestant somewhere in my ancestry that no one told me about. Didn't that coffee make you ill? I threw up.' He stopped talking suddenly, because he realised that it was Dougie's presence that was making him so garrulous, and the realisation made him self-conscious.

Jean said, 'We were just talking about whether it was better to be here or in Rhu.'

'Look out the window,' Dougie said.

Adam did, at the purple haze of birches and the glow of the dead bracken and the soft green of the stones. 'You can't eat scenery,' he said. Dougie laughed at that, and Adam said, 'I have to go. I'm supposed to spend Monday afternoon on the phone to the nursery.' As he was putting his boots on, he said to Jean, 'Did you ever think of the Open University?'

Jean said, 'Dougie keeps telling me that. But I don't think I have the brains.'

'You might surprise yourself,' he said.

As he came back to their house, he had a glimpse through the window of Norah moping at the kitchen table. But in the time and noise it took him to come through the porch and take his boots off she had found something to do, and had her hands full of sheaves of paper as though she were tidying them away. He smiled at her, and she smiled back weakly. 'Where have you been?' she said, and then justified it by saying, 'The nursery phoned.' She was trying to make herself sound normal.

'Walking,' he said. He wanted whatever had been going on to stop.

Telling her that he had gone out to prove her insanity wouldn't have improved matters.

She said, 'We used to go for walks together.'

And then he exploded. 'That was three days ago. We went for a walk on Friday. If you really want to know what I was doing, I called on the Millars to see if Jean was in a state about last night, and apologise to her. But I didn't need to. She seemed to think it was perfectly normal.'

'You used to tell me the truth,' she said.

'I am telling the truth,' he said. 'What's all this "used to" business?'

He realised that he had been shouting by the silence that followed it, and then, while picking at the table with her hands, she said in a quiet voice, 'So what were you telling the Millars about me? That I am stupid and hysterical?'

'You were never mentioned,' he said. He was leaning across at her, red in the face, with his eyes bulging, shouting again.

She said, 'Why are you so angry all the time? Why do you hate me?'

'For Christ's sake,' he said. 'You win. Take your fucking coil out. If you having children is a condition you make for us leading a sane existence, then I agree. Just leave me alone, will you?'

She had to leave the room for a few minutes to work up the courage to tell him, and when she came back she stood in the door as if she was ready to run. 'Adam,' she said.

'What?' he said impatiently. He couldn't bear to see her standing like that, in a way that suggested he might be capable of violence. As if she knew nothing about him at all.

'I had the coil taken out last spring.'

And then he began to laugh. It was a giggle at first, and then he bellowed with laughter, until tears came streaming out of him.

Adam developed the habit of taking his morning tea out on the shore. He had his bath before Norah, and brought her coffee in hers, and then, while standing in the kitchen with the tea in his hand, he would find that there was something in the atmosphere of the house that was pushing him outside. It unsettled him to be standing about, waiting to see what mood Norah would be in once she was dressed and ready, with nothing to do. Things had not been right since the night he had talked to Dougie. His first instinct was to load everything into the car and get them away from Inverclachan, but from all accounts the house in Herefordshire had been made completely uninhabitable by the builders. He decided to wait, in silence, until it was possible to go home.

On those mornings he never stopped to put a coat on, because he always thought that he was only going out for a moment, and because he found the cold pleasurable. He would wander first down as far as the shore, mug in hand, and as often as not he would find himself wandering along it, placing his feet on the grassy hummocks because he was shod and not booted. There was a heron that would fly up and land on a stone in the middle of the loch to watch him. If the tide was out he could walk a long way, to a part of Inverclachan that was inexplicably known as Canada. It bore a slight resemblance to a prairie; or maybe it was something to do with the Highland Clearances. Perhaps it was from there that the people of the region were loaded on to cattle-boats at gunpoint before being taken to Canada. It was exposed and empty and no houses could be seen from it, except for the small cottages on the other shore of the loch. It would have been a good place for lovers to be met or mourned.

Sometimes he would be gone ten minutes, and sometimes he would be gone for the morning. The odd day he called into Shore Cottage on his way back to see how the Millars were, still with a blue mug in his hand. Their house seemed more comfortable than his own. Once, he was there when Lucinda Goodlands called in. She seemed shocked to see him socialising with her personal paupers, and conversation was difficult. The talk turned to cheese, and Lucinda said, 'I don't think that any house should be without Stilton.' Adam looked at Dougie, and Dougie was retreating towards the bedrooms to suffocate his laughter in private, and then Adam tried to catch Jean's eye, but Jean had turned towards the sink so that Lucinda wouldn't see her smiling.

About the beginning of December, Adam came back particularly late from a walk. He had been talking to Dougie, who was clearing scrub, up by the flagpole, and then he had walked on, to the limits of the estate. It was one of the days when he saw things clearly, and he made up his mind that the Inverclachan thing had gone on too long. He missed his garden, and he missed Norah's companionship. He thought that living on a building site had to be better than living in this state of limbo. He almost ran, back down the hill to tell Norah.

The smell of dope hit him as he came into the house, and he knew that there was a visitor, and he knew which visitor to expect. Paul and Norah were sitting at the kitchen table with an empty wine bottle between them. Norah had a somewhat glazed look about her. 'Darling,' she said. 'Paul wants to know if we will go to the Oban Ball with them.'

Adam said, 'Really? Can anyone go?'

'Well,' Paul said. 'Not the pastoral people.'

Adam would have liked to catch Norah's eye, but it was plain that she had been smoking dope and was away with the fairies. Instead, he saved the remark up to tell to Dougie. 'No,' he said. 'I didn't mean that. I thought you had to have a tartan, and a clan and stuff.'

Paul said, 'I'm sure we can fix you up with a kilt.'

'That's very kind,' Adam said. 'What is the Goodlands tartan?'

'The Goodlands wear the MacLeod.' Paul made it sound as though it should be a privilege for the MacLeods.

'Wonderful,' Adam said. 'I like a bit of dancing.'

He was trying to be as cheerful as he could; trying not to notice that the woman sitting at the table bore no resemblance to the person he had fondly imagined as he was rushing down the hill. Norah said, 'There is a parcel for you from the nursery. I didn't open it.' She had taken to saying this about his mail, as though he had secrets which she had every right to know about, but which she chose to ignore.

'How will I ever forgive you?' he said.

Paul said, 'So you are off to Ireland?'

'Only for a few days.' Adam looked at Norah, trying to gauge how much and what she had been telling Paul. 'It's for a christening. People keep producing children.'

'How lovely for you,' Paul said.

Adam said, 'Yes.'

'And poor Norah will be all alone.'

Adam said, 'Norah can come if she wants to. She doesn't like Ireland much.'

Norah said, 'I do.' She was contradicting him out of petulance.

'Well, come then,' Adam said.

The telephone rang in the next room, and Adam went to answer it. He had hoped that by the time he came back Paul would be gone, but he was skinning up another joint, running his fingers over the paper to smooth it. Norah looked at Adam in a meaningful way to make it clear that she wasn't going to ask who had phoned.

Adam said, 'That was Thomas.'

'His brother,' Norah said. 'In Dublin.'

Paul said, 'How lovely.' It wasn't clear whether he was referring to Adam's brother, or the joint which he was twisting the end of.

Adam said, 'It's trouble with my father.' He thought he could see a glimmer of response from Norah, but he knew that this wasn't the time or place. 'I'm going out,' he said. Paul was offering the joint to him, but he said, 'No thanks. It's wasted on me. I can't inhale. I expect Norah will have a bit more after I've left the room. Where is that parcel from the nursery?' He put a coat on, and took the parcel and a trowel, and went out of the back door and up the hill towards the flagpole.

Dougie was on his boulder, rolling a cigarette with his back to the wind. Adam said, 'Those are bad for you.'

Dougie said, 'Sit down,' as though they were in a drawing-room and Adam's visit had been expected. Adam sat the other way from Dougie, facing the loch, and so making a sort of love-seat of the boulder. He told Dougie about love-seats, and Dougie inhaled on his cigarette, making a sort of smile at the same time. The smile might have been just a method of inhalation, or it might have been a smile.

Adam said, 'We can't sit out here all afternoon. Come out to Glen Dubh.'

Dougie said, 'Why?'

'Just do.'

As they were walking up through the woods, Adam said, 'Paul was below in the house. I can't deal with him at all.'

Dougie said, 'So you've worked that one out.'

'Something came up, and I was about to tell them about it. Paul and Norah. But it was a bit of a nightmare. So I came up to tell you instead.'

Dougie said, 'Thanks.'

'Well, I won't if you don't want me to.'

Dougie said, 'I only want to know why it involves a two-mile hike.'

'It doesn't. This is just killing two birds with one stone. The walk will do you good. And also, I had to bloody walk out here to listen to you rattling on about your life.'

Dougie said, 'I thought you implied that people like you didn't have problems. It was only us paupers.'

Adam laughed. 'Poor thing.' Then he said, 'It isn't my problem. It's someone else's problem that I am being dragged into.'

They reached the upper end of Glen Dubh, and Adam unwrapped his package. He took out six or seven pieces of root bound in peat and plastic and began to dig with the trowel. Dougie said, 'What are they?'

'Cimicifugas.' Adam spoke with the irritation that garden people have in their voices when they have to explain something.

'Of course they are,' Dougie said. 'How incredibly stupid of me not to have known.'

'Sorry. They are tall with nice white flowers and they like to live in the woods.'

'Isn't this going against your principles?' Dougie said. 'I thought you had a theory that Inverclachan was anti-gardening. That it was too perfect here to plant anything. Is this an attempt to mar perfection?'

'A few cimicifugas never marred any place. It was the only thing that was needed. Even God can't think of everything.'

Dougie said, 'It sounds to me as though you're getting delusions of grandeur.'

'It goes with the job. In any case, if they aren't meant to grow here they will die. God can still have his say. Planting things is only making suggestions, in the end.'

Dougie said, 'I can't argue with you.'

'That's what most people find. It isn't necessarily a good thing.'

Adam went silent. The sun had come out and lit up the glen at a slant, so that the westward side of the trees turned yellow, and seemed translucent, as though the light was passing through them. He could remember the last time he had been there when that had happened, and he was watching Norah climb about on the side of the hill.

Adam and Dougie were walking back, and they were laughing about something, when Adam said, 'My brother just phoned, and he has set me up to go into something called confrontation therapy with my father.'

Dougie said, 'What does that involve?'

Adam said, 'How would I know? I thought you might be able to tell me. You're the one who has seen more psychiatrists than anyone's had hot dinners. I thought I was going to Ireland for a christening, and now I have this loaded on me. Apparently the old man has chosen just this moment to put himself into a clinic. I suppose I've got to tell him what a bastard he is.'

Dougie said, 'It's hard to imagine that you have a father.'

'Not everyone,' Adam said, 'is blessed with a dead father like yourself.'

Dougie sucked air in through his teeth, like a mechanic making an estimate, and Adam said, 'Oh dear, I don't know why I'm saying this, but I can suddenly see how easy it would be to break your heart.'

Dougie said, 'I hope it won't come to that.' Adam was shocked by the seriousness with which he said it. The only thing he could think of to do was laugh in a nervous flirtatious way, and say, 'You'd better watch out, so.' But still he got the feeling that what had been a joke to him was something that touched a nerve with Dougie.

When he spoke again, it was as much to extricate himself from this as to unburden himself. 'Do you know? I don't know whether this is profound or not, but it struck me with a great blow. Does that make it profound? I was wondering, as I came up the hill to you, what I could possibly have to say to that man. I told my brother that I had nothing to say to him, and he told me to say just that. I can't see it doing any good. I have killed the man off in my head. How do you confront a corpse? I haven't thought about him for years. That's not the profound part. The other day, out in the cave, when you were talking about your dead father; no, not about that, about your fatherless life, and I was being all clued up and sympathetic. To be honest I thought it was very magnanimous of me to listen to someone as fucked up as you.'

The path they were taking was narrow, and Adam was walking in front of Dougie. He could feel that he was expressing himself in the wrong way, and he turned to look at Dougie's face for some idea of a reaction. But Dougie was impassive, or seemed impassive. His eyes were a darker colour and there was a slight wateriness to them, but that might have been the wind.

Dougie said, 'What can I say?'

Adam said, 'No, that isn't the point. That is just the way it was. You knew the dangers of talking to someone like me, who you hardly knew. In any case I assume that you were talking for your own benefit and not mine. And it worked out. That's fine. Fuck you, Dougie Millar, I am trying to be honest.'

Dougie said, 'I know.' There was still a wateriness to his eyes. There was no wind blowing and his face remained impassive.

Adam said, 'I have been going about these weeks, haunted by the things you told me, without knowing why. And then I was walking up the hill to you to tell you that my brother called. I was floundering through the reeds on the short-cut, and it hit me. It hit me so hard that I would have had to sit down if I hadn't been in the middle of a bog. I couldn't work out why I had no pity for you, and then I understood. I envy you. Your mother hated you, and so you are free of that. I had a mother who loved me and understood me, and just at the moment when she had raised my emotional expectations of this life to their highest, she went and died. She has spoiled every relationship for the rest of my life. No one can live up to a dead perfect mother. I wouldn't even dare to ask it. But even you. If you became a close friend of mine I would expect the sort of love from you that would rip you to shreds.'

Again, Dougie said, 'I hope it won't come to that.'

'And my father,' Adam said. 'I know nothing about my father. I don't want to. If I go for a few years without seeing him I can be almost fond of him. But being in his presence makes my stomach churn with acid. And that is only polite occasions, the weddings and funerals. Filial mutterings between mouthfuls of smoked salmon. And now they want me to confront the man.'

They had reached the flagpole again, and were looking down at the roof of Adam's house. Dougie said, 'What exactly is wrong with your father?'

'Oh that.' Adam kicked the boulder. 'He is an alcoholic.'

'Sound man,' Dougie said. 'I wish I was.'

Adam said, 'You'd have to be more plausible to get away with it. My father is very plausible.'

Dougie said, 'I can believe that. He has a very plausible son.'

'That isn't the sort of thing you are supposed to say.' Adam nodded down towards the house. 'Will you come down for a dram?'

Dougie said, 'Is Paul Goodlands going to be there?'

Adam said, 'I can't guarantee that he won't be.'

'In that case,' Dougie said, 'I'll leave you to face the wolves on your own.'

In the days that followed Norah was sullen. It was a state he had come to expect her to be in just before one of his visits to Ireland, but normally things would have come to a head. There would be a row, and the air would be, perhaps not cleared, but positively charged. In those few days he could not find the energy to indulge her by fighting. It was easier to wander out of the house and along the shore, until he felt himself become calm again. Sometimes it would take him three-quarters of an hour; sometimes it would take him to the Millars.

Dougie Millar aside, he usually found something to calm him in these wanderings, even if it was only the cold wind passing through him, or the onset of rain. He came to crave the cold, and deliberately wore fewer clothes, even though it aggravated the beginnings of rheumatism. He also came to value the feeling of his stomach being empty more than the satisfaction of it being full, and began to avoid meals. He would have been alarmed by this apparent madness if it had been new to him, but he recognised it as the pattern of his behaviour during the last few years he had lived in the same house as his father. In those days it had been impossible for him to eat in his father's presence.

He said to Dougie, 'It's me or him. I can't allow that man back inside my head.'

Dougie said, 'What can I say?'

'What do you want to say?'

'Calm down, Adam.' And then Dougie said, 'I hope it's you who wins.'

When Adam returned to Norah that day she greeted him with her new catch-cry: 'I just want to know what is going on.'

'Going on where?'

'Going on here,' she said. 'We used to live together. I hardly see you any more.'

'Don't be ridiculous. You see me for between twenty and twenty-three hours of the day.'

'You don't talk to me,' she said. 'When you are here, your mind is somewhere else. You behave as though you want to be somewhere else.'

As he was looking at her, he could feel his face breaking into a smile, and then a small laugh. 'Are you trying to ask me if I am having an affair? On Inverclachan?'

She was too far gone to see the funny side of it. 'All I know,' she said, 'is that you are behaving like someone who is in love.'

He said, 'I suppose I could have an affair. It would give you something real to worry about. We would have to move from here, though. None of the women on Inverclachan with loose morals are my type.'

Now she was crying. He said, 'You used to laugh at my jokes, and now you are crying. How can you criticise me for not talking to someone who cries at my jokes? So, you tell me. What's going on?' He put his arms around her, and he said, 'We have to get away from here. We have to get back to work; back to not having the time to think.'

And she said – do you know what she said? – 'After the Oban Ball.'

He tried. Can you see this? It kills me to write about it. They married each other not only because of love; but because it had seemed that they wanted the same things in life. And once they had achieved those things the small unspoken differences that had been pushed to the edge assumed monstrous proportions. She had a fantasy that, once they were alone together, the romantic side of him would come out; he would court her and flirt with her and she would be pregnant and content; he would pay her the small obeisances that her father had always paid her mother. She had always imagined that he was dependent on her; and in some ways she still thought that she had a chance of making a conquest of him. So that when she fought him, she was trying to wrestle him to the ground, and she did it with a single-mindedness that prevented her from seeing that what she was trying to do was impossible. She could only alienate him. And

111

who can say that she wasn't right? If she had been happy to carry on for ever with the half-love he was prepared to give her, perhaps she would have lost him in the end anyway.

And Adam. How can we have any sympathy for him? There was some fault in his character that made him inhuman. He was prepared to destroy anything that threatened his mental status quo. And who can say that he wasn't right? It might have been an instinct for self-preservation and no more. He might have known that if he let go of himself he would be annihilated by it.

The day he went to Dublin she refused to drive him to the airport. She said that the motorways around Glasgow would be too much for her, and so he had to take the bus from Achacloaigh. Buses made him feel sick. But it was one neurosis battling against another. If a neurosis is a weakness in itself, is it the strongest neurosis which wins, or the weakest? The answer is perhaps that the best-manipulated neurosis will win. He took the bus and she was saved from the motorways.

Thomas Parnell, his brother, was leaning against a pillar in Dublin airport. Adam approached him with an apologetic smile.

'Half-past three, me arse.'

Adam said, 'The plane was delayed.'

'I already figured that one out. Come on.' Thomas led the way, but towards the bar, not the exit. There was to be all the usual stuff about mountains of Guinness before you could even leave the airport.

'What are you having?'

'Mineral water.'

'You have to drink something. What are you having?'

'I have a headache. Mineral water.'

'Just the one pint.'

'I want water.'

Thomas said to the barman, 'Two pints of Guinness there, whenever you're ready.'

Adam added, 'And a mineral water.'

When the stout came, Adam left his untouched, didn't even acknowledge its arrival. Thomas drank both pints in the end. All this was normal, a ritual. Adam was irritated by being home within ten minutes of arriving. He couldn't see why it had to be like this. Why his own brother had to play the Paddy to him. Thomas made a cloud of cigarette smoke in front of his face, and through it he looked at Adam directly for the first time.

'So?' he said.

Adam was tempted to say something sarcastic; blow the whole thing and get back on the plane to Glasgow. But he realised by the way his brother was looking at him that 'So?' had been an honest question. Or as close to honest as his brother could get in the first ten minutes.

Adam said, 'So how are you?'

His brother said, 'Ahh,' and made a face. 'You know yourself.'

Adam could think of no response to this. He realised that he had lost the ability to communicate in his native language. He fished the slice of lemon out of his water. 'I hate lemon in water,' he said. And then he realised that Thomas was probably only playing the Paddy in response to him playing the worldly sophisticate.

Thomas said, 'So how's Norah?'

'Well, I think.' Adam tried to meet him half-way. 'It's hard to say. You know yourself.' He thought then that he had achieved something, and that he could ask a real question. 'What's supposed to be happening with the old man?'

'You'll see for yourself in a minute. Come on.'

The Tenbury Clinic was in Portmarnock, not far from the airport. They drove straight there in time for visiting hour. At the traffic lights, Thomas would take nips from the bottle of duty-free vodka which Adam had brought. 'To get rid of the smell of the stout,' he said. 'I don't want to drive them all wild.'

Adam said, 'Do we have to do this therapy thing straight away?'

'No. That's tomorrow morning. This is just visiting. They like you to have a visit first. If you can. I had to do the therapy thing last week.'

'How was that?'

Thomas made an agonised face. 'Ahh,' he said. 'You know yourself.'

The clinic was near the sea, in what looked like the remnants of the park of an old house. From a distance you saw a group of prefabricated buildings. It wasn't until you were inside that you realised there was a Georgian house at the core. Visitors were received in the basement, in what must have been the old kitchen, but was now a sort of common-room, filled with cigarette smoke and plastic furniture. Everything was stained nicotine-brown: the chairs and the people and the quasi-religious, uplifting posters on the walls.

The room was filled with people, in groups, smoking, and drinking tea. There was a table in the corner with an urn of hot water on it, and a bowl of tea-bags. Christian Parnell broke away from a group of people he was talking to and came towards them.

There was no sign of change in the man in the two years since Adam had last seen him. Physically he was an older version of Adam. The same hair; the same features; the same charm and plausibility. He didn't show his age, as though his life had been free of worry, which to a great extent it had. Adam forced a smile, and was offered tea and a cigarette.

His father said, 'Everyone smokes in here. People who never smoked in their lives are on forty a day after two days in here.'

Adam said, 'It's a good thing I'm not staying, so.'

Already he could see that his father was talking about the place as though he was only a visitor himself. Adam asked for a mug of hot water and a tea-bag separately. He dipped the bag into the mug once, but still it was undrinkable. One sip had made his stomach curdle. He thought at first it might have to do with the hideousness of the colour of the mug, but then his father began to speak again, and it was the same as in all the years between twelve and seventeen when he had never successfully ingested anything in his father's presence.

Christian said, 'How can you drink tea like that?' referring to the weakness of it.

Adam said, 'I can't.'

He was thinking that no one stood any chance of being cured in an institution as ugly as this, among these people. He watched the others in the room, trying to work out who were the patients, and who were the visitors. He decided that the alcoholics must be the relaxed ones, and the ones who seemed harassed and nervous must be their families.

Then his father spoiled his speculation by giving the case histories of everyone in the room, in a confidential mumble, and a tone of voice that implied that they all had problems which had no reference to himself. 'Do you see that one over there? The fellow who could do with a haircut? A terrible case. Beat his wife for fourteen years and there she is visiting him.'

Adam was tempted to say something about his wife being fortunate enough to be alive to visit him, but he let it go. He had made no reference to his mother in his father's presence since her death, and he didn't feel in the right frame of mind to start now.

His father carried on. 'Drugs too. He'll take anything. But not as bad as the woman behind him; the one in the dressing-gown. She marched out of the therapy yesterday and off down the road. She won't last.'

Thomas said, 'And you?'

Adam looked at his father as much to say that he had wanted to ask the same question.

Christian answered with an air which both implied that he was offended to be categorised with the other patients, and that he was manfully prepared to take whatever was coming to him. 'Oh, it's hard. I won't deny it's hard. You spend most of your time writing essays about yourself, and then they read them and tear you apart in the sessions. The sessions are terrible. Yesterday that man in the glasses over there had one of the counsellors by the throat, and sometimes chairs go flying across the room: everything. That one over there, in the beard and sandals. He is one of the staff. He called me a liar yesterday. Straight out. He said that I hadn't spoken a word of truth since I came in here.'

Adam knew, by the hard-done-by tones in his father's voice, that the whole thing was a waste of time. It struck him that perhaps after all these years his father had no other way of speaking about himself, but Adam had enough instincts left over from his childhood still to disbelieve automatically everything the man said.

He realised that Christian Parnell was in an impossible position. If he really did mean to get hold of himself and quit drinking, it would depend on everyone he knew giving him the benefit of the doubt. And anyone who knew him would have been mad to trust him. Adam found himself examining his father's words and actions microscopically, and he decided that nothing had changed. It was obvious that the man was still trying to charm his way out of a difficult situation by pretending to be a good person. Adam thought it was just as well that he wouldn't be seeing much of him; that he wouldn't be around for the next betrayal. He pitied Thomas, for his optimism.

Later, in the car-park, his father had come out to see them away, and with a certain amount of humility, thanked him for coming.

Adam said, 'I came for the christening. This was a surprise.'

'I know. But thanks for coming here anyway.'

Adam said, 'It's costing Thomas a lot of money.'

'I know,' his father said. 'I know.'

They were standing together while Thomas turned the car around. Adam was glad that he was leaving in a moment, because he could feel himself weakening; in danger of falling for his father's friendliness. The only thing he could do to save himself was to remain cold. He tried to think of something cold to say.

His father said, 'And how is Norah keeping?'

Before Adam could stop himself, he said, 'Not so well. For some reason she wants to start having babies.' And then, as abruptly as he could, he asked, 'Have you ever thought about committing suicide?'

'Often,' his father said.

And that was a shock. Adam made for the car door and escape. He couldn't deal with the idea that he could have a real conversation with his father. Something he had vowed never to attempt, for the sake of his own sanity. Once, when Thomas was seventeen, his father had engaged him in what Thomas had thought was a real conversation. They were talking about girls, and his father asked him, in a confidential way, if he had slept with any yet. Thomas fell for it and said that he had. And then his father threw off the cloak of friendliness and began to scream at him. It wasn't to do with morality. Morality was the excuse. It was to do with Christian Parnell proving to himself that no one was up to his standards. That even his own sons betrayed his image of himself. Adam had never fallen into that trap. But he always had the advantage of seeing Thomas getting it wrong, and tempered his behaviour to avoid the worst of his father's behaviour. Now, for the first time in his life, he had said something to his father without thinking it through in his head first; and to get out of it he had followed it up with a stupid, blunt and hurtful question. And he was surprised to find his father still talking to him; answering his question. And shocked that his father would admit to something as weak and human as a suicidal impulse.

Adam could say nothing. Getting into the car was a difficult moment from a physical point of view. He had the impression that his father would have liked to embrace him. But Adam had just about held himself together, and he felt that there was no need to risk spoiling it with familiarity. And there was something about the place too; all the psychiatrists at their windows would probably have liked to see them embrace. There was no need to play along with their megalomaniac fantasies. And it would have been a lie. You should not embrace someone who has not had the courage to embrace you since you stopped being a malleable child and started to become a person. At about the age of three.

That evening, Adam and Thomas got drunk together for the second time in their lives. As children they had disliked each other, and it had always been one of their father's habits to lecture them on getting along better. He had said once to Adam, 'Why can't you be like normal brothers? I would love, it would be the best thing, if one of the days the two of you fell in the door together drunk, with your arms around each other.' It wasn't long after this that it happened, and he and Thomas got talking, and got drinking, and fell in the door together laughing. Their father was furious; purple with rage. He behaved as though each of them had cuckolded him in some way. That was when Adam realised that their father had been one of the elements setting them against each other all their childhood. Christian Parnell's wish for reconciliation between them had only been his way of salting the wound. But perhaps this is harsh. The man may not have been aware of what he was doing. But a victim will tend to be more concerned with effects than motives.

In the intervening years, Adam and Thomas had developed an irritable liking for each other. And when they found they had nothing else in common, they could at least be united against their father. Now seemed as good a time as any to get drunk again. Adam drank an equal mixture of gin and Southern Comfort, something he had not done since he was twenty, and as a consequence was by far the drunker of the two by the end of the evening. He must have been, because Thomas drove them home, while Adam could hardly see his hand in front of his face. Thomas talked about cars for most of the evening, and Adam listened, because while he knew nothing about cars he found it comforting to be talked to, and because Thomas spoke as though cars were important to him.

When they got back to Thomas's house, Caroline, his wife, said to Adam, 'By the way, there is a box of stuff got sent up from Wexford that belongs to you. Liza found it when she was clearing out the attics. She said you might want it. I put it in your room.'

Adam's mind was in no state to deal with the fact at the time. He was concentrating entirely on holding himself together until he got to bed. Instead of answering he attempted a smile at Caroline to show that he had heard her, and then returned to the problem of whether he should take water to bed with him or not. He knew that he would need it in the middle of the night, but he also knew that he was bound to spill it on the stairs on the way up. In the end he half-filled two pint glasses, and mounted the stairs very slowly, taking the last part on his knees.

He slept a few hours and then woke thirsty. When he had drunk some water he found that he couldn't sleep again, because of a pounding in his ears and a grinding in his stomach. After a while he remembered the existence of the box and turned the light on.

It was mostly rubbish: old diaries and an old pair of secateurs. There was also a file of old letters that he began to read through. It all dated from when he was sixteen or seventeen. And then there was a page from a letter that his mother had written him, when he had first left home for a while, and just before she became ill. It was ordinary enough, but in among the ordinary things there was the sentence, 'I wish I could have done better for all of you.'

It might have been the drink, or it might have been the circumstances, or it might have been that the letter would have had that effect in any case; but he felt something pulsing through his body, like electric shocks, and he felt his face screw up and his teeth grind against each other, and lumps of sobs broke out of him and into the pillows. At first there were no tears, but they came in time, and he was two hours crying before he could fold the letter and put it away again. It was a strange thing for him. He hadn't cried at her funeral, or at any other funeral he could remember. The odd aria well sung in Covent Garden had elicited token tears in the corners of his eyes; but, in the fifteen years since her death, this was the first time he had lost control of his grief. He was only glad that Norah wasn't there to watch it.

In the morning Thomas was having a big fry-up. Adam dipped a tea-bag once into a cup of hot water, and then stared at it, unable to think about raising it to his lips.

'I am getting old,' he said. 'Drink doesn't agree with me any more.'

'Just as well,' Thomas said. 'The head?'

'The head is fine. Gin and Southern Comfort would never give you a head. That was the whole point of it when I used to drink it. It's the stomach.'

Thomas said, 'I'm a head man myself.' He was shovelling black pudding and aspirins down his throat. Watching him made Adam feel worse. His brother had gained a lot of bulk in the last ten years, and lost a lot of hair. These days he looked much like any Dublin businessman with a paunch drooping over his trousers. Adam watched him, thinking: Never. It will never happen to me. He put his hand on his own stomach, just to check, and thought about eating less, as a precaution. Thirty-three was a dangerous age.

Later, when Thomas had gone to shave and put a tie on, Caroline said, 'Well, at least he's better this week than last.' She was jiggling her new baby in a random way, as if she was mixing a cocktail. The baby seemed to be enjoying it.

Adam said, 'Why? What happened last week?'

'This same thing. This therapy. He was in a terrible state before it last week. And for four days after. He had to take time off work to get over it. It took a lot out of him.'

Adam said, 'I don't know why he's doing it.'

'We all have to try. You can't just do nothing.'

Adam said, 'You could put a bullet in him.'

Caroline was waving the baby around like a toy glider. 'Who do you think she looks like?' she said.

Adam looked at the baby. To him it just looked like a baby. They were all more or less the same. Some even more hideous than others. 'I think she looks like me,' he said. 'It's just as well you asked me to be the godfather. It will be nice for her to look like her role model.'

Caroline snorted.

Adam said, 'I am only doing this for Thomas. Not for the old man. If I tell the old man the truth or whatever it is I'm supposed to do today, it is for Thomas's sake. He seems to have some faith in the whole thing. I have a feeling he is going to be hurt by it. I gave up on the old man a long time ago.'

'Well,' Caroline said. 'Whatever you think yourself.'

Thomas came in and said, 'If this thing finishes on time we can make the second race at Fairyhouse.'

They crossed the city and drove up the coast towards Howth.

Thomas stopped the car at a pub just short of the clinic. 'Hair of the dog,' he said.

Adam said, 'I hope you have enough money left to put yourself in afterwards.'

'Jesus, you know,' Thomas said. 'That worries me. Sometimes.'

BOOK THREE

All right. This is perhaps the time to begin. Time to stop treating Adam Parnell as though he was only another character, and as though by some special dispensation I could see the workings of his mind. I can admit it now, and if Adam Parnell seems despicable then I am prepared to take responsibility. It wasn't only shyness. I could never have begun this if I was writing in the first person, and so I let you think that I was some sort of ghost, gazing out of the windows of Inverclachan House at the buckthorns and the loch. Perhaps you thought that I was Joshua Goodlands. That might have been my fault. I always liked his name. It was my original intention to pretend that the narrator was Joshua, but only because of the sound of his name.

And I am some sort of ghost; and I am gazing out of the windows of this house, and it is an extraordinary day. The water in the loch is as smooth as oil. But the name of this ghost is Adam Parnell. Do you know him? He was once a famous nurseryman. He was also once part of an entity, known as Adam and Norah. Now he is back in possession of himself again, for whatever that is worth. It is right that I wrote about him in the third person so far, because it is only now that I can see who he is. He could be worse.

Until that day in Dublin, whenever I dreamt of my father we were screaming at each other. Loud ferocious screaming with anger behind it. Norah would say, 'You were having a terrible dream.' And I would say, 'Was I? I wonder what it could have been about?' Do you see? I wasn't lying to Norah. I was avoiding any attempt to explain to her what I couldn't begin to explain to myself. Something I couldn't acknowledge. Those dreams stopped after that day in Dublin, and that was a surprise to me. I didn't go there to get anything out of my system. As far as I was concerned there wasn't anything in my system. I approached it clinically, and with a hangover.

The hangover made things easier. To be suffering from that condition in a place where people are trying to overcome their drink problems, and to have to listen to lectures on the effects of alcohol: it was hard not to snigger to myself at times.

There was a cosy little lecture, just before the confrontation bit, given by a very uptight woman with a lot of crimson lipstick. She kept emphasising how anyone was free to ask questions; and saying how they were pressed for time, so that no one would ask any. She explained all the latest scientific thought on dependency-as-a-disease, with a lot of irrelevant facts about resistance to alcoholism among the Han Chinese, and some well-rehearsed jokes thrown in to convince us what a warm real human she was. Her audience laughed correctly and she beamed her approval at us. It was not unlike being back at school, with one of those masters who likes to think that he is good at his job.

I said, 'I have a question.'

Her approval vanished. It seemed that she didn't want any questions after all. As far as she was concerned she had already told us everything we needed to know. I was supposed to feel as though I had been impertinent to the schoolmaster, except, what with being grown-up, and Thomas having paid an enormous fee, I knew that I could get away with it.

'Yes?' she said.

'What if,' I said, 'what if a person is an alcoholic because he is inadequate in the first place? You have spoken about the physiological and subsequent psychological effects of alcohol, and the shambling wrecks that alcohol produces. As though alcohol was the beginning of the problem. But what if that person was a shambling wreck in the first place, and became an alcoholic for that reason? What if, by curing someone of the drink, you are only removing the chief symptom of their real condition? Is this possible?'

She said that it was possible, and she looked at her watch, and then resigned herself to patiently explaining that it was sometimes possible to go into analysis or on to further treatment once the dependency had been dealt with. But that an alcoholic was someone who was poisoned, and you had to remove the poison first. Then as a matter of form she asked if there were any more questions, and I kept quiet, because I could tell that she wasn't going to tell me what I really wanted to know. The answer wasn't written on her clipboard.

An exceptionally stupid man with phenomenally large feet and a Liberties accent asked a very stupid question next, slipstreaming, so to speak, in the wake of mine, and I could see why she resented the questions, and felt sorry that I had started it. The man with the feet couldn't understand her perfectly lucid answer to his question, and went on repeating it until she said that that was all she really had time for, and left the room.

And as I was going through the building towards the prefabricated room where the confrontation was to be, I could see traces of what must have been nice rooms once, and the irritation of that was enough to keep me from thinking until I was seated again.

Leaving architecture aside, I found myself sitting on a plastic chair in a circle of twenty people or so. My father was more or less opposite me, and Thomas was two places to my left. There was a very self-satisfied man with his jumper tucked into his jeans who seemed to consider himself in control of us all. He wore ostentatiously small spectacles, and sat sideways-on in a way that could only have been interpreted as a subconscious desire to display his backside to us. I am not normally given to that sort of simplistic sub-Freudian analysing, but I think psychiatrists are fair game, don't you? Perhaps the poor man had piles, but whatever it was that made him sit in that odd way, it was no joy to look at him. His sidekick, who was on the other side of the circle beside me, was the one with the beard and sandals who had been in the common-room the day before. He had that unpleasant sort of intensity about him that made you think he spoke Irish at the drop of a hat and didn't wash. I remember thinking that the whole thing would have been enough to drive me to drink.

There was a revolting ceremony to begin with, where everyone had to introduce themselves to the group and say why they were there. I heard my father say, 'My name is Christian and I am an alcoholic.' At that moment I felt like leaving. Perhaps making a dramatic exit. To hear the truth from someone who usually tells lies makes you cynical. And you think that he isn't necessarily saying it because he thinks it is the truth. If he lies about everything else, he isn't saying it because he believes that he is an alcoholic. He is only saying it to save himself hassle. I wanted to say, Oh, come on: if it was as simple as that. Do you seriously think that you can wriggle out of your life by eating humble pie and taking on the mantle of a shameful condition? You've had thirty years of bed-making, you fucker. It's nearly time you had to lie in one of them. But I remembered Thomas on my left, and I kept quiet for his sake.

When my turn came, I heard myself repeating the formula, 'My name is Adam Parnell, and I am here for Christian.' I slipped my surname in as a little rebellion. A spanner in their chummy works. The backside-displaying psychiatrist glared at me, but I was too busy thinking that it was the first time I had ever referred to my father by his first name, and I took no notice. Saying the name 'Christian' seemed like a transgression of something. Like in the Old Testament when they talk about uncovering your father's nakedness.

My father tried to smile at me. I grinned back at him, hoping to give him a false sense of security. The backside-displayer, still glaring at me, fixed a professional smile across the lower half of his face and said, 'Well, Adam. Would you like to start?'

I was struck dumb. I had assumed that someone with some previous experience would start us all off, and I would have time to consider my tactics. I didn't know whether the man was doing it out of spite, or whether he knew something about psychology that I didn't. Eventually, trying to suppress my irritation, I said, 'Well, do give me some sort of clue. What sort of thing do you want me to say?'

The backside-displayer smiled triumphantly, and with a practised condescension asked me a leading question or two. It was an effort to ignore my personal revulsion for him and concentrate on the job in hand. And then a coldness came over me, and I found myself saying exactly what I thought. The words came out of me with no emotion attached to them. And at the same time I watched my father's face, as impervious to the expression on it as a cat to the terror on the face of a vole.

I said, 'Well. I am perhaps a bad choice as the person to begin this with. Because really I have nothing to say. But I had thought of one small thing, which, perhaps, is relevant. I have a friend, and a while ago he was in a bit of a state, and began to tell his troubles to me. Among other things his father committed suicide when this chap was a child. At first I tried to be sympathetic to him, until I realised from the things he was saying that he had got as much goodness out of his dead father as I had got out of my supposedly live one. Perhaps this is too abstract a concept for this situation, but the most painful thing I have had to deal with in my life with my father is to have believed in the existence of a man who did not exist.'

I got the feeling that nobody in the room had understood what I was saying, except my father. The psychiatrist turned, to expose his other buttock, and interjected, 'How does this relate to alcohol? Could you talk about some of the ways in which your father's alcoholism affected your life?'

I said, 'I don't see what alcoholism has to do with it. I have never known my father when he wasn't an alcoholic, and so I have no way of separating his behaviour from alcoholic behaviour. I suspect there was always something inadequate about him. If he hadn't taken to drink it could have been something else. And as for how it affected my life: my life is fine. Mostly because a long time ago I learned to behave as though my father didn't exist. I have killed him off in my head, and so I have survived.'

The backside-displayer made a small sound of exasperation. He said, 'You might talk a little bit about your father's behaviour at home.'

'What? Juicy details? I don't think there are any. He was never a drunk. I am not aware that he was ever violent. He is a very plausible man, as you yourself must know by now. The disruption he caused was more subtle than that. A whole childhood of depending on someone who doesn't exist, who is completely unreliable and too selfish to be capable of love. Being asked to be loyal to someone who had no loyalty to you, and being too young to understand what was going on.'

'Can you think of some incidents?'

'Well, of course I can. But I can't see how relevant they are. They seem petty compared to the real psychological damage that was being done. We were always short of money. My mother used to have to sell her furniture to the tinkers to buy food for us. All that sort of thing. On the one hand it was embarrassing, but on the other she saw to it that we never went hungry. That might have been a pity, in a way. If it hadn't been for my mother mitigating the effects of his behaviour we might have worked out what he was like a long time before we did. The trouble was that she believed in him, and we were prepared to believe what she believed.'

'Are you saying that your mother acted as a barrier? How do you feel about the way he treated her?'

'I am saying that our mother loved us. That is not always a good thing. It leaves you without the equipment that is necessary to deal with a person like my father. Being loved is not a betrayal in itself, but it sets you up for betrayal. My father treated my mother abominably. But that isn't something for me to talk about. He knows all that already. I don't really like to talk about my mother while he is here.'

'Do you blame your father for your mother's death?'

'No.'

I was looking at my father now, while I talked. He was weeping. Because he was weeping I found it easier to be cruel. He was more easily despicable. I quite wanted to put him out of his misery.

'No,' I said. 'But there is something which is perhaps worse. I often think that if the alternative was a life with him then she is better off dead. She used to speak about death with some fondness, as if she was looking forward to it. I think she must be happier now.'

The displayer said, 'Christian. Do you have anything to say now?'

Everyone looked at my father, who was slumped forward in his chair. His face was ugly and swollen with tears. I found him irritating.

He said, 'I am sorry.' He repeated this several times, shaking his head.

I said, 'Oh, for Christ's sake, what's the good of that? It's a bit late to be sorry. To pretend to be human. The time when anyone needed you is long gone. You can spare me that "sorry" shit. If you want to be sorry for anyone you might as well just carry on being sorry for yourself. It should be quite a habit by now.'

He pulled himself together slightly, and he said, 'I am sorry because I did love you, and it seems now that you were unaware of it. That is my fault. I want to change that. I love you.'

He nearly got me there. He nearly had me in the same state as himself. But I knew. I knew from years and years ago that this was not a man to be trusted. I was grateful for the cold blood in my veins, and without even allowing my voice to quiver, I continued.

'So? Fuck's sake, what does that mean? That means nothing to me. How can I be loved by someone I don't believe exists? I am not going to start believing in you again. If you want to try your hand at being human, the best of luck to you, but don't expect me to get involved in it. I've been there and done that. We've all been taken in by you before. I suspect that Thomas has been taken in again this time. But you're not having me. If you want to do this, go ahead and do it for your own sake. The way I feel about you now, I am quite safe and sane, and I see nothing from here that makes me want to change my position.'

My father said again that he was sorry.

Of course then they brought Thomas into it, and it seemed that the week before Thomas had told our father that he hated him and blamed him for our mother's death; but this week there was a lot of schmuck about love and Thomas got weepy too, and I was so irritated that I wanted to scream, but that wouldn't have done any good.

When they finished with Thomas, they moved on to the next little family, and I couldn't really see why we had to stay, but it seemed that leaving wouldn't have been the thing to do. It didn't seem fair that no one spoke honestly after my turn; they told lies and repressed things and played the victim for all it was worth. I couldn't see hope for a single one of those people. Their minds were too small to save themselves. And I began to sympathise with the attitude I had seen in my father the day before, when he was holding himself apart, as though he wasn't really a patient. I looked across at him again, and seeing that he seemed a little hunted, I smiled at him.

I drifted off into a small fantasy about controlling my father. About keeping him in a wee cottage somewhere near by, on a small allowance that wasn't quite enough for drink. Just thinking about the slight humiliations in it, like the humiliation of being a child and having to ask for things. To turn the tables and treat this man the way he had treated me for seventeen years. I could develop such an air of martyred disappointment in him, and make him feel as worthless as he was.

I was brought back to the proceedings by everyone standing up and joining hands in a farcical way, and chanting an uplifting slogan to bond us all together in spirit. I felt more ridiculous than I ever had in church, and almost as ridiculous as I do among salespeople.

And then my father walked across the room to thank me. I almost asked him if he hadn't a shred of dignity left in him, but instead I said, 'Don't. There is nothing to thank me for. I meant it.'

He said, 'I know. I am going to try to make it up.'

I said, 'To me? Don't bother making anything up to me. I'm fine the way I am. I would have thought you were going to have enough trouble making it up to yourself.'

We had been walking out of the building while we were talking, and once we were outside my father lit a cigarette and looked away towards the windows. He said, 'Yesterday, after you left, they called me in and gave me a roasting. They had been watching me say goodbye to you, and they said it was too friendly and cheerful.'

I wanted to tell him that it was because he was too charming and plausible. That no one had any option but to disbelieve everything about him, but instead I said, 'That's because they are gobshites. They don't know how civilised people behave.'

And still I didn't embrace him when we said goodbye. Perhaps if I had, I wouldn't have dreamt the dream I dreamt that night. An embrace might have dispelled the physical tension between us. That night I dreamt of my father erotically. Well, not that it was very erotic for me. He raped me. I found the whole thing a bit peculiar and disturbing, and I haven't dreamt about him since. I never got to tell him that he raped me in a dream, or got to see what he would have made of it. It must be very odd if your father makes love to you. Much odder than him not loving you at all.

The thing about Inverclachan is that if you go away from it for a few days it is impossible to remember quite how extraordinary it is. When you come to the bend by Shore Cottage you have to stop the car for a moment, and then drive on slowly, among the rocks and the mosses and the small bare oak trees, the hills sliding down into the far side of the loch and the Islands drifting out across the sea. It is no more a place you can describe than a place you can remember. The only analogy I can think of is making love after a long period of celibacy. The best aspects of it are only apparent while you are experiencing them.

The sole drawback on Inverclachan is the people. I would like to seal it off from them and leave it to the otters and the deer. The people intrude. I even came to resent the ferry that passed down the loch twice a day as an intrusion. Norah loved to watch the ferry going by, and I ground my teeth. And at the same time I was intruding. I found a place on Canada where I thought *Sanguinaria canadensis* might thrive, and I planted some out. It seemed like an irresistible idea at the time. I half-regret it now, but I would still go down there to watch them flower in April among the birch scrub. And it is hard to stop that sort of thing once you start. I smuggled some *Gladiolus tristus* bulbs into a sunny hollow behind the flagpole, and I've lost count of the amount of *Salvia uliginosa* I have scattered here and there. Perhaps I have done this place more harm than good. But I have found that the trouble with being human is that you can't leave things alone. We are an intrusive species.

So, you return to Inverclachan and to begin with you are stoned on the scenery, until you see a walker in an orange waterproof, or Paul

Goodlands and his dog traipsing around, and then you are sobered; or Norah says, 'Well, and how were your family?'

'Fine. They send their love.'

'So you were talking about me?'

'No. They just send their love. They managed to remember that I was married to you all by themselves.'

And once I was back inside the house with Norah, the first thing I did was to go into the kitchen and open a canister of tea and push my face into it, breathing deeply.

Behind me, the ever-anxious Norah said, 'What's wrong? What's the matter?'

'Real tea,' I said.

I don't suppose, in all fairness, that she ever found me very easy to live with, or to understand. Not that I ever asked to be understood, only to be trusted.

And when they asked me about my father, both Dougie and Norah, I gave them the same answer, in the same tone, 'I told him that as far as I was concerned he didn't exist.'

Norah put her arms around me, and said, 'Oh, my poor darling. I'm sure you didn't mean it.'

There was nothing I could say to her. After a few days away from her the only thing I had to express was my lust, and maybe it was then that I realised for the first time that sex was the only thing left between us. I left her sleeping on our bed and washed my hands and left the house, and went wandering away to find Dougie.

Dougie said, 'So what did he make of that?'

'I don't know,' I said. 'I can't win. If I think for a moment that I am being unfair to him that gives him power over me. And if I am right then there is no hope for any of us.'

Dougie said, 'What can I say?'

'Tell me to calm down. I've been looking forward to that.'

Dougie said, 'Calm down, Adam.'

Christmas came to us before things could get worse, and Norah and I did all the things we had always done at Christmas: had hen pheasant on toast for breakfast; dinner in the scent of a bowl of forced General De Wet tulips; big fires and Benedictine. All those things made Norah happy and allowed me to seem happy. It was only the parties we had to go to that made us fight. We agreed that we would be perfectly happy if we never saw anyone else at all, but still we went to the parties.

The Oban Ball was the exception. That was awful enough for us to be united in our view of it. Thousands of upper-class colonialists pretending to be Scottish, and fat Scottish businessmen pretending to be upper-class colonialists. Luckily you could spend the whole evening dancing, and not speaking to anyone, or when you were tired you could go and eavesdrop on inane youngsters boasting about their public schools; and it was amusing to watch the arrogance of the people in kilts and shot silk who knew that they were beautiful because their forebears had bred for years with beauty in mind, and the more extreme arrogance of the ugly people whose forebears had bred for wealth. Whenever anyone began a conversation with me, I asked them straight away how they felt about nationalism, and half of them hardly knew what the word meant, and the other half went away after I had expressed the view that the only good thing about the word queen was that it rhymed with guillotine. I thought that Dougie would have been proud of me.

And I wore the kilt that the Goodlands had lent me, although there was a strong debate about what to wear beneath it, and Lucinda said that Paul always wore his boxer shorts and only yobs wore nothing.

And after that Norah was pro boxer shorts; but I asked Dougie and he set me straight, and I think he must have been right, because after the Oban Ball it seemed to me that yobs were the only real Scottish people left. So I sided with the yobs, and indeed, you can only reap a lot of the benefits of wearing a kilt if you wear nothing beneath it. The sweat from your dancing drips straight on to the floor and you stay cool and dry beneath. And the other great advantage became apparent in the car on the way home, and you only have to move your sporran a bit to the side for the kilt to seem a very practical garment, given the right partner.

So, that was fine, but in between Christmas and the New Year something fell away from us again, and she fell back on her catch-cry, 'I just want to know what is going on.'

I said, 'There is nothing going on, except that plainly I am making you miserable. I can do nothing to help you. It is up to you to decide whether you can survive by living with me, and if you can't, then you must leave me. But I don't want any more of this drama; this emotion that means nothing. If I am making you neurotic, then leave me, but don't make us hate each other with your neurosis.'

This conversation was at about five in the morning of New Year's Day. We had just come back to Joshua's cottage and I was in the kilt again, although this time it didn't seem to be having the same effect on either of us. There had been a dance for the New Year on Dunbeag, two miles down the road. It was fine until midnight, and midnight was fine, and the dancing was wild and much better than the dancing at the Oban Ball, and people wore T-shirts with their kilts and had a good time. And after midnight I said to Norah, 'I'm just going away for half an hour. I'll be back.'

'Where are you going?' she said. You would think I had just told her I was emigrating.

'First-footing.'

'You are going to Shore Cottage.'

'It's a tradition,' I said. 'Do you want to come?'

She refused with an air of moral superiority, as if I had suggested something obscene. 'You do what you like.'

If you drink a lot of whisky, and dance at the same time, you can't describe your state as drunken. It is more lucid than that, more euphoric: you have more motor control. I can remember driving a lot faster than I would have driven if I was sober, and I must have been driving well, because on those roads there is no allowance for bad driving. I am making no excuses for drunken driving; but in that place at that time there was no one to be killed but myself if I crashed. I squared it with my conscience, and it was more like flying than driving.

I must have been a little over-excited when I swept into Shore Cottage, knocking on the door as I went through it. Dougie and Jean were bemused; they stood and looked at me with indulgent smiles. Jean's parents, who were staying, had already gone to bed. I said, 'It's wonderful. Come up for half an hour. You'll love it.'

Jean said, 'I don't think I can remember the dances.'

I said, 'You don't need to. I didn't know them at all until four nights ago.'

She said, 'We won't know anyone.'

I said, 'Neither do I.'

Dougie said, 'Are the Goodlands there?'

'No,' I said. 'They went home long ago. I think Lucinda is still sulking because she was thrown out of the Oban Ball for breastfeeding in the bar.'

Dougie said, 'All right, we'll go.'

I knew they would. There are times when you can impose your will on people by sheer enthusiasm. And I think they enjoyed my new style of driving, although Jean was very silent in the back.

It turned out that Dougie couldn't dance at all. He made half an attempt at the Hamilton House and then went to the back of the hall, by the drink and Craig Anderson. I didn't get to go and talk to them, because between the reeling they played rock-and-roll and so I was kept busy; but I could see by Dougie's face that he was consuming a fair bit of whisky. He was engaging two lads out from Glasgow in a conversation that seemed animated even by Glaswegian standards, and whenever I spun near them I overheard enough to know it was about nationalism.

At about four I noticed that he had disappeared, and I asked Jean, with whom I was dancing, if he had gone home. She said she didn't think so. She thought he was in the room out the back.

I said, 'Oh dear.'

When I went to investigate he was unconscious, stretched across a billiard table. I went back to Jean and said, 'Look, this is my fault.

I'll get him home for you, and then come back for you and Norah. You stay and dance.'

'Fine,' she said.

Once he was woken, Dougie was in a violent state. He asked me what the fuck I was doing, and I said that I was taking him home.

'Oh, you are, are you?' he said. 'I can fucking walk myself. Get to fuck, you.'

So I let him try walking, and he collapsed on the floor, and I picked him up again and put his arm over my shoulders and half-carried him out of the hall. He swore at me the whole way, and made an ineffective attempt to strangle me as I put him in the car. But once we were driving, he said, 'Adam Parnell. You're the man for me. You'll show them. You'll show the bastards. Adam Parnell.'

He was still expressing these sentiments, more or less, in a fairly repetitive way, when we pulled up at Shore Cottage, and I hauled him out and got him in his front door, and I was about to propel him towards his bedroom, when he caught my head between his two hands and pushed his tongue into my mouth. I had never been kissed by a man before, and it was a bit of a surprise when it happened. It does have several things to recommend it. He didn't pussyfoot around the way a girl would, and he was the same height as I was, so there was none of that uncomfortable bending over. But the stubble was a bit hard to take. It was like being kissed by a Brillo pad. Still holding on to my head, he leaned back and looked at me carefully, and when he had taken in the expression on my face he began to laugh in a maniacal way, which I found, if anything, more unnerving than the kissing.

'I think it's time you were in your bed,' I said.

That made him laugh again.

'And you can find your own way into it,' I said. 'I'm off to pick up Jean. And if you keep laughing like that you'll wake the children.'

I left him leaning against the range and went back to the car. Half a mile from Dunbeag I met Norah and Jean walking along the road towards me. I picked them up. The atmosphere was strained: I thought at first I might be imagining it, because of what I had just been through.

It was just after we dropped Jean off that Norah screamed, 'I just want to know what is going on.'

A fight was fine by me just at that moment. I wanted to take my mind off other things until I had digested them.

'This isn't normal,' she said. 'Jean was in a terrible state. She didn't know where you and Dougie had gone.'

I took a very deep breath. 'Jean seemed fine to me,' I said. 'And she knew exactly where Dougie and I had gone because I told her before I left.'

'Well then, I don't know what's going on at all,' she said.

'Fine,' I said.

We reached the house and went inside, and carried on fighting in the kitchen.

'This isn't normal,' she said. 'Normal people don't behave like this. Who, in their normal life, has all day, like you and Dougie, to brood about their past and sit up in the woods talking?'

'So?' I said. 'We are not normal people. Is that such a bad thing? Normal people watch television and vote Conservative and eat Pot Noodles. Is that the lifestyle you hanker for? You never told me. It was your idea to come back here. Normal people don't spend their winters in the Highlands with nothing to do.'

'Don't be stupid,' she said. 'You won't advance your case with stupidity.' And then she added, in a voice that wasn't screaming any more, 'I wouldn't mind having a television.'

'Oh, Jesus Christ,' I shouted. 'Get a television. Get one for every room. That isn't the point. And why are you screaming at me?'

'I'm not screaming. You are.'

'You are.'

'Why do you hate me?' she said.

'I don't hate you. Why are you screaming at me?'

'You never talk to me any more,' she said.

I almost answered her. I almost said that I had never talked to her. It was only that she had never noticed before. I might have said it, but she had continued screaming.

'You walk out of this house without saying a word to me. You come back with some sort of elation about you, and then after one look at me your expression changes, and you are miserable again. You never tell me where you are going or when you will be back. You have secrets.'

'Where could I be going? I never know when I am coming back. I don't even know that I am going out until my feet are walking out

139

the door and I am outside. What is the point of living in a place like this if you can't go outside? But this is stupid. So what are you worried about? There are no brothels or pubs within walking distance of Inverclachan. What are you so jealous of?'

She said, 'Don't say that you don't know where you are going. You go and talk to Dougie.'

'Sometimes,' I said.

'So you talk to him about me. What do you tell him about me? That I am hysterical and stupid? Do you laugh about me with him? He must have a very twisted picture of me by now. I think it must have been him who poisoned you against me in the first place. I hate Dougie Millar. We used to be happy.'

'I know.' But that wasn't enough. I said, 'What is this about "happy"? I don't know of one married couple who are happy in the way that you expect us to be.'

'Dougie and Jean,' she said. 'Aren't Dougie and Jean happy?'

I said, 'How much do you know about them?'

'What are you saying? Jean really loves Dougie. She is really fond of him.'

'I am only saying that people aren't always what they seem.'

'What are you doing? You are interfering with them. You are ruining their marriage to amuse yourself.'

'Stop being so fucking romantic,' I said. 'The Millars' marriage has nothing to do with me. You are such a bloody snob. You think that just because people are not your sort they should behave like merry little peasants with uncomplicated lives. Paul and Lucinda can be as unhappy as they like, but the working classes are obliged to fit into God's scheme of things.'

'You don't know what you are doing down there,' she said. 'If Dougie leaves Jean and those children it will be your fault.'

'Dougie isn't going anywhere. And if he does he has a mind of his own. The Millars can think for themselves, you know.'

'Why can't we be happy again?' she said.

'That is up to you. I am happy.'

'But you aren't happy with me.'

'This is all in your head.'

The fight was going out of me. I wondered if she was right. The evening had been too bizarre, and I had realised that I was fighting with her for the enjoyment of it. Like driving the car too fast; I was doing it for a sense of power and control. I said, 'Look. This isn't any good. It is much simpler than this. You have to decide if you love me, and then you have to decide if you can go on living with me. I love you and I want to live with you, but I don't want to make you unhappy.'

She said, 'So why do you?'

And still neither of us could fight over the real issue. Since she had told me she had taken her coil out the subject of children had become unmentionable. We had to fight about other things instead. Things she had invented.

She said, 'Are you in love with Dougie?'

Of all the nights she could have asked that question. Perhaps she had an instinct. Perhaps she could see something that I couldn't.

'Oh, come on,' I said. 'We don't have to descend to that level.'

She said, 'I am old enough to know the signs when someone is in love.'

I began to laugh. The pressure was off. I should have told her that I wasn't in love with anyone, but that would have included her, and the fight would have gone on. I realised that she had spoken because the fight had reached that stage where people run out of real things to say and rummage around for absurd accusations. It can be dangerous at times, because people look for these accusations among their deepest fears, and so from time to time they strike home, unluckily. So far, I had wondered occasionally if Dougie had fallen in love with me; but there was no danger of it being the other way round. I laughed again at her, and even kissed her. Our fight was reaching the sexual stage, and I lifted my kilt to dry her tears in it.

So? Was that a watershed? I don't think so. The act perpetrated by Dougie and the question asked by Norah were coincidental. The former worried me more than the latter. The more I thought about it, the more it seemed obvious that Norah had insinuated homosexuality in an attempt to frighten me out of my friendship with Dougie. It was a measure of her desperation that she had done so. She thought she was losing me. Perhaps she was, but that was something between us, and nothing to do with how I felt about anyone else. I can see why, when a marriage begins to go on the rocks, it is so tempting to have an affair with someone else. It must simplify things and make them tangible. You don't have to flounder around in the darkness trying to work out what has gone wrong, and how things can be put right again; you only have to say, There is someone else, and you have a clean break; everyone will understand such a straightforward motivation. There are great allowances made for falling in love, and none at all made for falling out of it.

I could see it, but I wasn't going to do it. I wasn't going to let anyone off the hook by pretending to be in love. I didn't want anyone else; and if Norah was going to leave me, which was something that occurred to me more and more, then I wanted to be on my own, answerable only to myself.

The Dougie Millar thing was a more complicated issue. I had become fond of him, and his company. I was trying to suspend judgement until I had spoken to him and gained some idea of his motives. It might just have been that he was checking me out, or it might have been an outrageous drunken joke. It might only have been affection. But I had been teasing him about falling in love with me, and I might have taken things too far. You can't discount people's suggestibility, no matter how well you think you know them.

I was spared all this on New Year's Day. I must have drunk more whisky than I realised and I was incapable of movement, let alone thought, until the early afternoon. Norah brought me freshly squeezed orange juice and stroked my forehead. She had always been fondest of me when I was incapacitated. We had people coming to supper in the evening, and I managed to be out of bed by then, after a lot of aspirin.

I wondered if Dougie would come and see me, or whether he would be avoiding me. I thought it most likely that he would have no memory of it at all, which would put me in a difficult position. It would be impossible to continue any sort of friendship without talking about it. On the other hand it might be impossible for him to continue a friendship if we had to discuss it.

Both pairs of Goodlands came to supper. Paul was looking more porcine than usual; Lucinda was on her brightest behaviour, which unfortunately brought out her most suburban aspects. As he drank more, Paul began to wince visibly every time she opened her mouth. They had married while Paul was still a free-thinking hippy, before he became a squireen in tweeds. And my friend, Joshua Goodlands. I wondered if he would have gone the same way as Paul if he had stayed to live at Inverclachan with nothing to do all winter but smoke dope. I don't think so. He had some sort of vitality about him, and I was glad to have him there to talk to. And Jane: I haven't worked Jane out after ten years of knowing her. It is that fey aristocratic battiness that you never know whether to take seriously or not. She was telling us about her psychic brother, and how he was marked out to be special from birth because he was born with his umbilical cord around his neck. I said, 'Really? I was born almost dead of strangulation from my umbilical cord.'

She turned full towards me and opened her eyes like a stage medium, and said in a breathless voice, 'Then, you are surely an angel of God.'

Do you see what I mean? You don't know whether to laugh or what. The most important thing is not to catch anyone's eye. I said that I had always understood it to mean that I was to die of strangulation, but that sort of goriness wasn't in her philosophy and she carried on talking about angels and her brother.

Later, for some reason or other, I was left alone with Paul. Lucinda and Joshua had gone to fix one of the lavatories or something, and Jane and Norah had closeted themselves in the sitting-room. Paul, who was well in his cups, so that his face was even redder and his eyes were small slits, said, 'I've tried it all, you know. But I've found in the end that you can only trust people from your own peer group.'

I was too busy trying to work out whether he was including me in his peer group to answer him, and so, perhaps thinking that I hadn't heard, he said it again two minutes later.

'Trust them with what?' I said.

'As friends. Also in business. I have found that only people from one's own background won't let you down.'

'I don't know,' I said. 'I get on with all sorts of people. Some of my best friends have even been to public school.'

He was too drunk to take that in. It crossed my mind that he might be warning me about my friendship with Dougie, but then I realised that it was Lucinda he was referring to. We had heard that he had been seeing the landed flame again, who was presumably one of his peer group since she owned a huge chunk of Scotland. Lucinda's background was a more modest portion of Essex.

'Oh dear,' I said. 'It must be very difficult for you, finding people who fit in.'

'Yes,' he said, in complete agreement. He was beyond irony, and began to skin up. I couldn't work out how he could burn such a tiny piece of dope while drunk and manage not to scorch his fingers. Perhaps years of doing it had deadened the feeling in them.

When I saw Dougie next, I said to him, 'Jane Goodlands says that I am an angel of God.'

Dougie looked at me, and smiled, and said, 'She could be right, for once.'

I find that sort of thing more flattering than alarming, of course. But just at that moment I was in the mood for a bit of cure-or-kill.

I said, 'Do you remember much about the other night?'

'Bits of it,' he said, smiling to himself.

'You were pretty obnoxious.'

'Was I?'

'I had a hard time getting you into the car. But once you were in it you were quite sweet. You kept telling me that I was the man for you.'

144

'So you are,' he said.

'And?'

'I seem to remember some French kissing,' he said. He said it very loudly, as if it was some sort of challenge, blowing smoke up his face so that he had to close one eye.

'That was the bit I had wondered if you would remember,' I said.

'Well?' he said.

We were in the sitting-room of Shore Cottage. The day was too fine to be inside. It made it hard to think, being indoors when you would prefer to be out.

'Come for a walk with me,' I said.

We went for a long walk that day, right off Inverclachan and up through the forestry and back along the cliffs by Dunbeag caves. It must have been seven or eight miles. Quite early on, my thoughts condensed into one question. 'I am only going to ask one question. Well, I am only going to ask one that you have to answer. I will probably ask a lot of other questions afterwards, but this is the important one. This is the question that affects whether I can bear to go on talking to you or not: Did you do it because it was something you wanted to do; or was it because you thought it was something I wanted?'

He walked on without saying anything. He seemed uncomfortable and a little angry. I said, 'Well?' and he said nothing, so I walked backwards in front of him, to needle him. 'Are you not answering because you don't want to? Or are you trying to think of the answer?'

Eventually, when he spoke, it was a minor explosion. It was also tinged with a disappointment in me that it took me a long time to understand. 'For myself,' he said. 'I did it for myself.'

'Well, that's all right then,' I said. 'That's the answer I can cope with.'

At the time I understood very little of the way his mind worked. It seemed healthier to me to make references to it and jokes about it. I would say things like, 'So long as it doesn't go any further. I don't think I could deal with the backside end of things, do you? So unaesthetic.' And I would be laughing, and he wouldn't be, but he would say very seriously, 'Me neither.' I had that lapsed Catholic attitude to sex that saw anything vaguely sensual as intensely and intrinsically funny; while his mind worked in a dourer way, and sex was something serious and silent, and strictly self-referential so that the other party had no say in the matter and no right to discuss it afterwards. Once I had worked all this out I was quite pleased not to be gay. Dougie Millar would have been an impossible lover.

Over the next week there was a bit of a strain. He was silent and grim with me, and I was relentless in trying to tease him out of it, because I thought it was stupidity on his part to allow something as trivial as a drunken kiss to get in the way of a perfectly good friendship. It didn't occur to me that I was being misinterpreted, until one of the days up by the flagpole when he finally exploded and told me to leave him alone.

'Why?' I said.

'Because,' he shouted, 'I am sick of these seduction proposals.'

First it made me laugh, and I laughed so much that it made him smile too, and then when I had got my breath back I said, 'Well, hang on. Let's not forget who made a pass at whom. And if I have to go on about it, it is only because I have to find some way of dealing with it while remaining fond of you. And the last thing I need at this moment, even if you were a girl, is to have an affair with someone. What I always liked about you was that I got everything else from you except that nasty sex stuff. With Norah, sex seems to be about the only thing we have left in common. That is no basis for a relationship.'

Because I had never said this out loud before, once I had said it, I had to stop and think about it again, and I tried to disprove it in my own mind. But I couldn't see that it wasn't true. There was nothing left between me and Norah but fighting and fucking.

Dougie said, 'Well, that's all right then.'

And it was. That was the closest we got to fighting, if you discount one-sided violence. After that I trusted him, not because I was sure that he wouldn't ever jump me again, but because I couldn't care less whether he did or not. And I think that might have been his idea when he stuffed his tongue down my throat in the first place. He was laying the ghost that haunts all men who are friendly with men.

Back home, I wondered whether to ask Norah if she thought that we did have anything left in common apart from sex, and I found that I couldn't bring the subject up, and I suppose that in itself was my answer. But she said one morning, 'I don't understand it. You are so nice to me in your sleep. While you are asleep you put your arms around me. You are quite affectionate. And then you wake up angry.'

'No, I don't,' I said crossly.

'There, you see.'

'That is because,' I said, 'we have nothing left in common except sex.'

And I expected her to be shocked, or to argue with me, but she only said, 'Don't say that. Don't make jokes like that. It upsets me.' And she began to weep quietly as she felt about on the end of the bed for her dressing-gown. 'Did you know,' she said, 'that Jane and Joshua are having a bit of trouble?'

'I told you so,' I said. 'There is no such thing as a happy couple.'

She ignored that, and said, 'Jane thinks that he might be gay. He gets letters from men that he won't show to her.'

'When did she tell you that?'

'The other night. In the sitting-room.'

I am normally bad-tempered in the mornings, I suppose, and it wasn't difficult to be angry. 'Why the fuck do you women do that? Why are you so afraid of men talking to each other? That isn't fair. You closet yourself in rooms with other women for hours and you keep each other's confidences and you weep all over each other and nobody suggests that there is anything odd about it. But as soon as a man talks to anyone except his wife he is either having an affair or he is a raving shirt-lifter. And it works. It fucking works. Most men are so terrified of that sort of thing being suggested that it works. Why don't you just buy us leads and collars and wee nametags?'

I was shouting the last piece of advice from the bathroom, just before I slammed the door. It was two hours later when she answered me, and we hadn't spoken in between. 'I suppose that men aren't to be trusted.'

'Are women?' I said.

She said, 'Don't be angry with me. I don't want you to be angry any more.'

'What are we going to do?' I said. She wouldn't answer me. I said, 'I don't want to do this again. When we get back I want to sack Graham and manage the nursery myself. I want to make it smaller, and close the garden to the public so that it is just for ourselves.'

She said, 'I am beginning to hate this house.'

'Are you? I thought it was heaven on earth for you.'

'It was. But I hate it now. I hate sitting here on my own. We could go back to Herefordshire early.'

'I suppose,' I said, 'we could.'

I didn't say it with any great conviction. I was dreading the return to Herefordshire. I felt it might be going backwards, and attempting to recreate something that might never have existed. We could spend the rest of our lives pretending to be happy for the sake of contentment. Up until that winter I had prized contentment above everything, but now I wanted to get as close to the truth of things as possible. I had begun to see that the truth was something that terrified Norah, and that was why we were drifting apart. Nor could I see that I could get it with anyone else. The idea of being alone began to appeal to me more.

Norah said, 'What are you thinking?'

And I said, 'Nothing.'

And she smiled and seemed happy. It was plain that I had lied to her, and that made her happy; and perhaps my thinking nothing could have made her happy too.

I said, 'Dougie and I had the most amazing walk the other day. We went up in the forestry and back by the caves at Dunbeag. There was a gorge with beech trees at the top of it that was completely lined with moss.'

She said, 'I don't want to know about that. I don't want to hear what you do with Dougie. You never walk with me any more.'

'How can I,' I said, 'if that is your reaction to the things I see?' But she was away on a sulk again. I said, 'All right. We can go now. We can do the same walk, and see the same things.'

So we went on exactly the same walk, and she seemed happy again, and I said, 'Why do you pretend to be so simple?' But she didn't understand what I meant. And we got to the gorge with beech trees, and she exclaimed and said how beautiful it was, and I remembered Dougie walking through it in an angry silence, which allowed me to look at it uninterrupted by purple exclamations. And every now and again Dougie would stop and stare at something and walk on again, without having to describe it. Norah made her exclamations, and I winced, and resented her for spoiling the sight of the gorge for me. But then I thought I was being too critical, and to make comparisons like that was unfair, and I remembered a time when I had loved her for her awkward schoolgirl verbal enthusiasm. So instead of walking twenty paces ahead of her as I usually did, I fell back and watched her walking and scrambling, and forgot about looking at the gorge, but looked at her, and I thought perhaps I did love her. She was always at her best in the distance, when she moved.

We had a few good days after that, and we even went to supper at Shore Cottage, and Dougie and Norah discovered that they had the same taste in awful early-seventies earth music, and they played Van Morrison and I don't know who else, and I drank too much and while we were walking home there was a full moon and I sang 'The Moon of Alabama' at the top of my voice, as if I was doing it because I was so drunk, but really it had something more to do with happiness.

But you see, my living father was waiting in the wings. I won't say that he had anything to do with it; he was just the next thing that happened.

After the cure and Christmas time, Christian Parnell did a grand tour. He had it in his mind that he should visit all his estranged children and demonstrate his new-found humanity to them. He was supposed to be coming with my second oldest sister Rosy, who was a medical student in Dublin. Because she could only have the weekend off they were staying just the one night, and it wasn't going to be much of a strain.

You can't say whether those things are coincidental, but at about the same time there was a bit of a crisis in the packing shed in Herefordshire, and it seemed that one of us should go down to sort it out. It was obvious that I should be the one who stayed behind, because it was my family who were visiting. But when I think back on it, it seems to have been a bit too convenient for Norah. Perhaps I am being unfair. Anyway, the thing was that she was to be away during my father's visit.

I am being unfair, because her being away was far more convenient for me. If I had to face up to my father it was going to be a lot easier for me if Norah wasn't around. I had more control of myself in her absence. Now that I think of it carefully, I may even have misled you. It may be that I encouraged my father to come the weekend she was away. I could have put him off until the next weekend without inconveniencing him or Rosy. But I remember thinking that it was better to face him on my own, with Rosy as an impartial referee.

I told Dougie that as he was my recently acquired father-figure he should meet my father. I amused myself by introducing them to each other in my head: Dad, this is my father-figure. Dougie, this is my father. I'm sure that you two must have a lot to talk about.

150

I drove Norah to Glasgow to get the train early on the Friday morning, and on the way back I stopped in the Great Western Road to buy food and drink. I went over the top with exotic fruits and vegetables; things I hadn't eaten since we had left England. And other luxuries you can't get in the Highlands like coffee beans and Parmesan cheese.

I couldn't work out why I was having no dreams of my father. I thought that, because I usually remember all my dreams, I was perhaps suppressing the ones with my father in them. On Friday night I tried that thing, you know, where you decide to remember all your dreams just before you fall asleep, but still, in the morning I had no recollection of him, only banal dreams of fighting with Norah.

Is it my fault, the feeling of well-being I had, once I was alone in the house? All Friday afternoon, I found myself not so much doing housework as minimising the household. Apart from cleaning and polishing I threw sacks of stuff out; and ironed and folded away every garment in sight (except anything belonging to Norah, which I just stuffed into her drawers, the way she would); and turned off all the heating and opened all the windows and doors and cleaned out the grates until the house felt and smelled of nothing but the cold clean air. I set a big fire in the sitting-room, knowing that I wouldn't light it until just before the visitors arrived. I did it all with the intensity and application of a criminal who is destroying evidence.

I had a bath before going to bed, and slept in clean sheets by the open window, with no one but myself to please, and no other body to make me warm and sticky, and I enjoyed it as much as you would enjoy a body to wrap yourself around if you had been sleeping on your own for a year. In the morning I woke myself up by singing in my sleep.

From time to time I would smell my hands, and there was something odd about them. And then I realised that they no longer bore any trace of Norah, and only smelled of themselves and soap. I saw this in neither a positive nor a negative light, but the novelty of it fascinated me all the same.

Saturday morning was spent just wandering through the sterile house, enjoying the silence. If I had to use a knife or a mug I would wash it again immediately so that there was never more than a ripple in the perfection of the place. I combed the cats and brushed the dog. If there had been a parrot in the house I would have preened it. And all the time the cold was invading me, until no part of me was warm, and I was content with myself.

The afternoon was for cooking. I was giving them a saddle of venison with sautéed potatoes; and a salad of fresh figs and kumquats and greengages to finish with. There were oysters to start with if they wanted them.

I didn't know if drink was going to be a problem. There was some very good Chianti classico I had found in Glasgow which I was looking forward to, but I didn't know if that was being unfair. In the end I remembered that my father had never been a man for drinking wine, and decided to go ahead with it.

I had miscalculated the time it would take to drive from Stranraer and they were several hours late, and apart from that there was a great awkwardness in the atmosphere. Once they arrived I resented them for disturbing my solitude; and they refused the oysters; and picked at the rest of their food until I asked them if there was something wrong with it, and they said, 'No, no, it's lovely,' and tried a little harder to eat some of it. When I produced the wine I gave my father a questioning look, and he said, 'No, no, that's all right. You go ahead,' with a benedictory tone in his voice. Rosy downed her first glass in one go and held it out again, and I said, 'Well at least you are thirsty.' They looked at each other in a guilty way, and Rosy said, 'We might as well tell him.'

My father said, 'We were starving. We stopped in that last town, what is it? Achasomething? And had fish and chips. Rosy said you would have supper ready, but we didn't know how much further it was going to be.'

'It doesn't matter,' I said. But I don't know if the tone of my voice conveyed the carelessness of the sentence. Now they were both completely embarrassed, and at the same time no longer felt obliged to pick at the food. 'Will you have pudding?' I said, but they wouldn't.

Rosy said, 'It's a very cold house, isn't it?'

'You get used to it,' I said.

They had coffee crouched close to the sitting-room fire, and Rosy consumed great quantities of brandy. I wondered if she was doing it deliberately, but my father seemed to take no notice.

'You are looking well,' I said to him. He looked pleased with himself, as if I had said the right thing. 'So,' I said, 'how is it going?'

'Ah,' he said, 'you know yourself.'

I said, 'I suppose it's early days yet.'

Rosy sniggered.

I knew that my father had come all this way with the vague intention of making up for thirty lost years, but I couldn't see how he was going to do it, and I decided to wait and see what he would do. With anyone else I would have suggested that he have a drink to oil the wheels, or I would have been able to have a drink myself; but one sip of the wine had curdled in my stomach, and I found even the smell of brandy nauseating. Rosy was quite relaxed by this stage, spreading herself out across the sofa and giggling at the two of us.

My father said, 'You don't have a television?'

'No.'

He said, 'So what do you do all day?'

'Read, walk. I do a lot of thinking. The world needs more contemplatives. I was supposed to be writing a book about shade-loving plants, but I haven't done much of it.'

'And what does Norah do?'

'She reads and walks.'

I realised that I was presenting our way of life as something that was incomprehensible to him. He was looking at me as though he couldn't believe what I was saying. 'So that's it,' he said. 'You just read and walk.'

After a difficult silence, he said, 'It's a very cold house.'

In fact the heat of the fire was too much for me, and I took my jersey off, and Rosy picked it up and put it on. It was too tight for her, and came down to her knees, but she seemed happy in it.

Somehow, the conversation got going. I can't remember any of it directly, but it was all that sort of meaningless amateur psychiatry, with my father using the jargon he had picked up in the clinic, and the subject of my mother came up, and Rosy said to me with a certain amount of resentment, 'Of course you were always her favourite.'

And I said, 'How can you say that? She never had favourites. I was always arguing with her because I couldn't see how she could be so nice to you when you were such an obnoxious child.'

'Me?' she said.

'You were awful,' I said. 'Nobody liked you except our mother.'

'You had a pony,' she said.

'Only thanks to myself. I wasn't exactly encouraged. I had to keep it a secret from him, or he would have sold it for drink. Which he did in the end.'

'You were too big for it,' my father said.

I said, 'That's no excuse for turning a good horse into catfood. And there were plenty of younger ones who could have taken him over.'

Now I had antagonised both of them, and they brought the subject back to my lifestyle and how it couldn't possibly be good for me to have nothing to do all day. I said that I had earned it by working for the last fifteen years or so, and gave my father what was supposed to be a very meaningful glance, and asked him if he had thought of anything to do himself.

And then he was like his old self again, and told us about all his latest Get-Rich-Quick schemes, and I could see that his grasp of reality was no better than it had ever been. He had spent his life thinking that a million pounds was about to fall into his lap.

I said, 'They said in the Tenbury that an alcoholic will always think like an alcoholic.' He looked wounded, and I said, 'Perhaps you should just get a job.'

'I would if I could,' he said.

'I could get you into horticulture. Plants are very addictive in a harmless way. You could become a hosta collector if you need an obsession.'

He looked at me incredulously.

'I'm serious,' I said.

Rosy said, 'Don't you have any way of heating this house?'

I said, 'It can be colder. When I am on my own I leave all the doors open.'

I think they decided that I was slightly mad, and I wasn't going to disabuse them. From what I could see, my father was acting a part and wouldn't be able to sustain it. I thought it would be healthier for me in the long run if there was some sort of barrier between us.

When I asked them when they would have to leave, they said eleven the next morning, which made the whole visit fourteen hours long, nine of which were spent asleep. I had walked through it feeling like a spectator, and if I half-wished that something would happen, I was determined not to make it happen myself. I watched my father for any signs that he would cross the barrier I had put up, and all that I could see was that he was lost.

It is complicated to have a relationship with a blood relation, if you have nothing in common, and thirty years of misunderstanding behind you. With almost anyone else you could at least break the ice and consummate things by fucking them. I was tempted to tell him about the dream in which he had raped me, but I knew it wouldn't have done any good. He had always been a bit of a prude in those matters.

There was a crisis at breakfast. I said, 'China tea, or Indian?'

'Have you no ordinary tea?'

'First-flush Darjeeling?'

'Tea-bags.'

I had to drive up to Shore Cottage to borrow some tea-bags from Dougie and Jean. I had to borrow sugar as well. It disturbed me to think that I had changed so much and become alien to my own family; until I remembered my mother making weak China tea, and her passion for it. I wondered then if it had been my father who had changed so much, and compromised himself, until I remembered that he was never there to notice my mother's passions, and that until recently tea was not my father's tipple.

He came with me to Shore Cottage, because I was going to amuse myself by introducing Dougie to him, but he stayed outside in the car, and the Millars weren't up properly, and so they never met.

I said to them, 'It's a bit of a disaster, and there is a rake of food that no one will eat. You had better all come to lunch.'

But Jean said that she had got some lamb for their own lunch, and I should come to lunch with them, and I said that was very kind but I shouldn't, and I happened to mention the oysters, and so Dougie said that he might come down for a drink in the afternoon, if there were oysters going.

After breakfast, my father lectured me about selling our car. 'It will fall apart with rust after a winter here. You should get rid of it before it becomes too noticeable.' He tried to make it sound like friendly advice, but there were years of fatherhood piled up behind it.

I said that we were fond of our car, and he looked at me as if I was mad, and I said, 'It is blue, and they don't make them any more.' And he made an impatient noise, the sort of noise a father makes when you come home with your hair cut in an inexplicable way when you are sixteen. Then he offered to tune it for me, or set the sprockets or something, and things got worse when I had to admit that I didn't know how to open the bonnet.

Rosy was uncharacteristically silent that morning: a background figure waiting for something to happen. I asked her if she was hungover, and she said no derisively, as if I had accused her of something shameful. The women in our family are rather less wimpish than the men.

Nothing did happen. They drove away in a dry storm, with the wind groaning in the sea buckthorns and carrying the salt from the tops of the waves in across the land. And again there was a moment of awkwardness when it seemed as if my father would like to embrace me before he got into the car. And I thought: Good grief, this man does love me; and then I thought: Well, and what does that have to do with me? That is his problem.

They left me unperturbed, and wondering what on earth they had come for. They left me clean and dry and hollow. I lifted my fingers to smell them. They smelled of nothing at all now; not of myself or even of soap. I wondered if I had not cut myself off too much for my own good, and if it was too late to go back. I felt as though nothing could touch me, and I was a little bit pleased with myself.

Once they were gone away I began to clean the house again, and left all the doors open so that the wind could blow away the smell of their cigarettes; and it was only when it was as cold inside as it was out that I began to feel comfortable in the house again.

The leftover food was an irritation. I would have liked to throw it away, but it is impossible for some people to throw good food away. I couldn't eat it, because my stomach was still in a knot, and even the idea of eating made me gag, but I thought that I might feed it to Dougie, and have the pleasure of watching him eat.

When everything else was clean, I had a bath and lit a big fire and put some vodka in the freezer and settled down to wait for my next visitor.

Dougie arrived saying that he couldn't stay long, but in the event he stayed until the early hours of the morning.

We started by the fire with oysters and vodka. I could manage the oysters by then but not the vodka, and Dougie said, 'I see you're keeping your wits about you.' And then he threw an oyster back and said, 'Is it true that these are supposed to be an aphrodisiac?'

And I said, 'You tell me. I've never noticed them have that effect.'

'So,' he said, 'how's your father coming along?'

'From what I can see he is close to the edge. Either that or he is inhuman. I can see that he might be inhuman. I don't feel too human myself. But he looks at me sometimes like a beaten dog. I wish that he wasn't my father. I could probably like the man. Did you know that? And did you know that no matter what you do your son will hate you? Even if he is unaware of it himself.'

Dougie said, 'I think he hates me already.'

'No,' I said. 'Not yet.'

After the oysters I gave him red cabbage and hot port, and I began to drink a little myself; and later still we had figs and brandy. Dougie ate the figs as if he was giving oral sex to a girl.

As he drank more he was inclined to become emotional, and then aggressive. In my cold detached state I watched this metamorphosis and wondered what the outcome would be, and went on filling his glass out of curiosity. The man had an incredible capacity for alcohol. By half-past eleven I had thrown up and was sober again, but Dougie went on drinking, and began to talk politics.

'When this country is independent it will need a leader. A leader will have to come from the people. Someone will have to be the King of Scotland.'

'I have no time for kings,' I said. 'If Scotland has a king, it will all have been for nothing.'

'From the people,' he said. 'A king from the people.'

'It doesn't matter. Power is intrinsically corrupt. A monarchy is necessarily an evil institution.'

'You don't understand what I am saying,' he said. I had thought until that moment that Dougie Millar was sane. He was looking at me with a film of water across his eyes.

'Are you proposing yourself as a candidate?'

He wouldn't answer me, but only went on looking at me through his sheet of water, as if I had hurt him. He was disappointed in me, because he had tried to reveal his biggest secret to me and I wasn't buying it.

'Do you think,' I said, 'that it is possible you are slightly schizo-phrenic? Just a small bit?'

'Fuck that,' he said. 'Get to fuck.'

'All right,' I said, 'tell me about it. I'm on your side. I don't know if I could like a king. But you have to risk that. If you can't trust me with it then you'll never be able to tell anyone.'

'Get to fuck,' he said.

'Why?'

'Why? If you can't see why you can't see anything. You can sit there and look at me as if I was a dog or something.'

'I'm sorry,' I said. 'Monarchy, as a subject, has that sort of effect on the way I look at things. It has to be up to you to convince me.'

For a long time he just looked at me, in a way in which, in other circumstances, I would have found unnerving. But in the previous days I had become so detached that nothing could touch me. After a while he said, 'There is nothing to explain. It just is. You should be able to understand. Adam Parnell should be able to understand this.'

I said, 'Perhaps I don't want to just yet. I usually have to have a bit of time to think about things. If Scotland has to have a king, I can see you might be the man for the job. I just wouldn't like to see what being a king might do to you.'

And then I had to be silent, because I was ashamed of myself. I was humouring the man as if he was a lunatic; and the fact was that, even if he was a lunatic, he was also a friend and deserved more honest treatment. I couldn't think of anything to say that was honest and wouldn't hurt him.

The telephone rang, even though it must have been after midnight. When I picked it up, Norah said, 'I thought you would phone me.'

'I've had my family here.' And then I said, 'That's ridiculous, you could just as easily have phoned me.'

'I didn't like to,' she said. 'Have they gone?'

'Yes.' Dougie began to walk around the room making whooping noises.

She said, 'What was that?'

I said, 'Dougie and I are getting drunk.'

'I knew you would be.'

'How's the packing shed?'

'Fine.' Our conversation petered out. I couldn't think of anything to say to her that I could say in front of a man who, even temporarily, thought he was King of Scotland. In comparison Norah sounded gloriously sane.

'Do you still love me?' she said.

I did a sort of affirmative grunt.

'Well that's all right then.'

When I put the phone down Dougie was flat on his back on the floor and snorting through his nose. He said, 'Adam Parnell; fuck you, Adam Parnell.'

I smiled at him.

He said, 'Adam Parnell, you're some man.'

I said, 'How are you feeling?'

'I could do with another drink.'

I went to get the rest of the vodka and some chocolates from the fridge, but I was thinking: If this doesn't make the bastard throw up then nothing will. When I came back he lunged across the room at me and picked me up by the jersey and slammed me against the wall. I wasn't struggling. I felt quite relaxed about it; detached from it, and wondering what was going to happen next.

So, picture this: a man, whom I have just deemed to be insane, has me pinned against the wall. There is spittle dripping from the corner of his mouth, and he is glaring into my eyes with all the anger that is in him.

I said, 'What is it, Dougie?' I had the feeling that nothing that was going on had anything to do with me. Dougie was behaving as though he were in front of a mirror, shifting his head slightly from side to side, and drawing it back slowly. I wondered if he was going to headbutt me. The kiss of the Gorbals. I suppose I should have been frightened, but I felt safe. I didn't think that he could touch me, no matter what harm he did to me. Is trust the word for that? Trust is the only word I can think of that fits: it isn't a question of what the other person will do to you, but of how you feel about it.

Then Dougie said, 'Get to fuck,' and dropped me on the floor and went back to the drink. He poured himself a glass of vodka and drained it with one swallow, and that seemed to jolt him into the next dimension.

I picked myself up and he came close to me again, but this time without violence, and spoke to me in a high-toned whining voice. 'Adam Parnell. Adam Parnell. Look at my eyes. What do you see? Look at my eyes.'

'Nothing,' I said. 'I see your eyes. What can I say?'

He became more aggressive. 'You're not looking at them. What do you see? Can you see me at all? Do you know who I am?'

I thought perhaps that I was supposed to say that I saw the King of Scotland, but as I didn't I wasn't going to say it. I said, 'I know who you are, Dougie Millar. Dougie MacLeod.'

He said, 'Liar. Who do you see in my eyes? Can you see anything at all?'

I could see nothing in his eyes but a reflection of myself, and then it dawned on me, and I said, 'I can see myself.'

'Ay,' Dougie said. 'Right.' He said it with the patient tone of a schoolmaster that he sometimes adopted with his children when they had been slow in realising something that he was explaining to them. I thought that now that I had answered the question correctly that would be the end of it, but after each slug of vodka Dougie would repeat the same questions as if he had never asked them in the first place. I got bored with answering and fell silent, and then the questions would increase in force until Dougie was shouting and screaming, and then he would fall silent himself and his eyes would fill with tears, and while the tears were still wet on his face he would start the questions again in a soft singing voice that slowly became harder and louder. I went on filling his glass, and he went on drinking from it.

In among the repetition, the content of Dougie's speech changed slowly so that Iain MacLeod's suicide was introduced. By now he couldn't see me at all, but was talking to his own reflection in my eyes, and this time I got the impression that he wasn't seeing himself there, but seeing his father.

'Bastard!' he said.

I said, 'Dougie?' I was speaking in the tone of voice you would use if you were trying to wake a sleeper. 'Dougie, did you ever want to try it yourself? Did you ever think about topping yourself?'

He drew back and focused on my whole face.

'Adam Parnell,' he said.

'Did you?'

He said, 'Of course I did. I thought about it so much that I couldn't do it. I tried it once but the bastards found me and pumped me out. In Fort William.' He looked at his father again and said, 'Some people have all the luck.' After that he couldn't see me at all, but carried on his conversations with the reflection.

I enjoyed being a cypher, and lounged in the chair with my eyes wide open, letting Dougie work his passions out. I was neither interested in what he had to say nor bored with it, but I was willing to participate.

He went to the lavatory and came back with a broom handle that had been left in the hall. He stood in front of me with it, twirling it above his head in a melodramatic way, and I watched. When it came whistling towards my head I dived out of the way by instinct, and the handle bounced on the back of the chair. In diving I had fallen to the hearthrug, and before I could get up again Dougie had jumped on me and rolled me on to my back. He knelt on my chest and held the broom handle across my throat.

I don't think I could have broken free of him if I had struggled. He had the strength of anger in him, and any movement I attempted made the pain worse on my throat. And so I allowed instinct to evaporate and made no struggle. To some extent I was flattered to be the object of such passion, in the way that when you are young you will sometimes allow people to sleep with you, not because you want to yourself, but because it is flattering to be desired. And then I remembered that Dougie was looking into my eyes, and not murdering me, but murdering himself or his father. And somehow, even in the pain of it, I found myself amused by my predicament.

And at one and the same time I had to ask myself if there wasn't something masochistic in my enjoyment of it. It had been a long time since I'd been so close to death. In my childhood I had loved hunting. The best moments were when the horse was going too fast to be checked before a big slippery ditch, and as you crossed it you would look down into the bottom of it and realise that in the next second you could be dead. The feeling you had wasn't anything like a thrill, but a great calm, the evaporation of all worry and neurosis. And if you fell, and the horse fell on top of you, you could keep your eyes open and watch the hooves crashing about inches from your face, and all you would feel was a satisfied calm. I felt the same calm with Dougie kneeling on my chest and the air blocked from my lungs. There was something desirable in being killed by a creature like a horse or Dougie Millar.

I thought that the next day I would wake up and find that I was a flying six-year-old child in search of his next parents, and Dougie would wake up to a sore head and murder charges. And I remembered the last conversation I had had with my grandmother. She was dying and she said to me, 'Oh, fuck this pain. I can't wait for me wings.'

'And your harp,' I said.

'They can keep the harp,' she said. 'I was never musical.'

The memory of that made me laugh, inasmuch as a man who is being strangled can laugh. The main manifestation of it was a contortion of the face which could have been taken for anything, but it meant that I closed my eyes, and Dougie lost sight of whatever he was trying to kill, and his anger collapsed. He stopped pushing on the broom handle and slumped across me, shuddering with tears. When I was able, I put my arms around the man and said, 'Never mind. No, no, at all.' I remembered those words from my childhood, and I tried to say them in the right crooning voice, but I could only manage a sort of crackle, but the meaning was clear, all the same.

Later I drove him home. He wanted to walk but I felt responsible for the state he was in and I thought I should see him safely to his door. He had sobered up a bit by then, and become affectionate.

When I called at Shore Cottage the next day I was on my way to Glasgow to pick up Norah. Jean was on her own, ironing and smoking and watching an Australian soap. She said that Dougie was still in bed, and I said, 'Never mind. I'll go through and surprise him.'

That was the first time I went into that bedroom. It smelled of marriage. How can I explain that? It is a sort of bland smell that you get when the distinctive smells of men and women mix. I had been sleeping in the same smell for years. It was noticeable to me now, after a few days without it. Dougie lay in the middle of the bed looking crumpled and hungover. He was wearing thermal underwear that he had slept in, and he rolled cigarettes without having to sit up.

I said, 'You want to give up that filthy habit.'

He said good morning to me without looking up and licked his cigarette paper. I said, 'How's the head?' and that made him smile, and then look up at me.

'What's the big scarf in aid of?' he said.

I said, 'What can you remember about last night?'

'Bits and pieces.' He reached up to me and fingered the scarf. 'That's not a Campbell tartan, is it?'

'I don't think so. I can't remember, but it wasn't Campbell. I got it because I liked the colour.' He made a cynical noise. 'You got in a bit of a state last night.'

He said nothing. He was pushing rolled-up cardboard into the end of his cigarette. I said, 'Aren't you going to ask me what you did?'

He said, 'I was assuming I was going to be told anyway.'

'Not if you don't want to.'

'I'm not buying that,' he said. I pulled the scarf off and stretched my neck out. Dougie inhaled with a hissing noise. 'How did you manage that?'

'You did it with a broom handle. When you weren't trying to crack my skull open.'

He examined the bruise and put his thumb out to touch it. 'Could you not have stopped me?'

'Not really. But I wasn't trying either. You were going to save me the trouble of topping myself one of the days.'

He said, 'Ay, and me in Barlinnie by now. Thanks a lot.'

'I thought you might as well be a prisoner in Barlinnie as a prisoner here. At least they might give you an education there.'

He said, 'Thanks a lot.'

I said, 'Are you always like that when you drink?'

'Not recently,' he said. 'They used to call me the Big Howler when I lived in Rhu. I used to get drunk on Monday nights and howl in the streets. Apparently. I don't remember doing it myself.'

I said, 'I expect the whole thing is a plot to discredit you.'

'Ay,' he said. 'I've thought of that myself.'

I thought about discussing his political aspirations, but decided not to. It was something I had to have more time to think about, and as it was I was perfectly satisfied by the discussion we'd had. It would seem that neither sex nor violence was to come between us. I asked him if there was anything I could get him in Glasgow, and he said, 'No, nothing that you could get.' And then as I was going out the door he said, 'You could bring me back some more of those figs. They're the business.'

And when Norah saw the bruise, she said, 'What have you been doing to yourself?' I thought it was odd that I could show people an injury that was plainly not self-inflicted, and still the first reaction of both of them was that I must have done it myself.

Norah was in a bad temper. But that was only the way with her. She had always met me with scowls after any period of separation, and we always had a little fight when we met. I assumed it was because the reality of me fell short of her image of me. I could understand that, since I did it with other people. But with Norah, once she had gone away I couldn't retain an image of her at all. I could remember her body, but I couldn't imagine her face unless she was sitting in front of me; and so I was generally pleased to see her after a separation. It filled a hole in my memory.

'Dougie tried to kill me when he was drunk,' I said. 'It was quite funny.' I wasn't just saying that. I was genuinely amused by the memory of it. Norah had no response at all, she didn't even look at me in an odd way. God knows what she must have thought. At the time I thought it was a perfectly normal thing to admit. It only seems bizarre in retrospect.

I do know what she thought. She thought that I was lying in some way. She had come to think that Dougie and I had secrets between us that we were guarding so closely there was no point in her trying to find them out. She was trying to keep hold of herself until we had left Inverclachan and she could resume possession of me.

She said, 'It seems we won't have to sack Graham after all. He's been headhunted. He gave me his notice.'

'By whom?'

'America.'

'Hostas?' I said.

'Hostas.'

'One of these days,' I said, 'someone will realise that there are enough hosta hybrids on this planet.'

'Not Graham,' she said. 'He's very excited about a new seedling which he says has all the qualities of *plantaginea* but with blue leaves.'

'He's been saying that for years. They never smell, and even if they did they are ugly. I can't see why people want to meddle with *plantaginea*.'

She said, 'We should go back soon. By February.'

I said, 'I'm not sure I really want to be a nurseryman any more.' I don't know if I meant it. It is one of those things you say as you are drawing the car up outside the house, and straight away you get out of the car and leave the other person floundering for a moment, until they follow you into the house asking if you meant it.

That made the rest of that day difficult, and silent. And I wasn't just playing games with her, I was playing games with myself. I was giving voice to half-formed ideas to see how they sounded. And in some ways I was trying to let her know that she couldn't depend on me, for the moment.

That evening Norah said to me, 'Do you want to change everything? Does this mean you want to stop being married to me as well?'

'No.'

She said, 'Is there someone else? You can tell me. I've been half-expecting it.'

'No.'

She said, 'So you are staying with me because you can't think of anyone else to be with?'

'No.'

'What, then?'

'Then nothing. If I wanted to leave you I would leave you. I wouldn't mind being on my own. Why don't you trust me?'

'Because you have secrets,' she said.

'I have no secrets. Sometimes I tell you things before I have thought of them myself. Everything you see is everything there is. I have never been more honest with you in my life.'

'Well, that's all right then,' she said.

It is impossible, once someone has stopped believing what you say, to expect them to believe even the most obvious facts. The simpler the truth which you present them with, the more devious they think the lie behind it must be. It had begun to amuse me, telling Norah the truth and watching her work out her own version of reality. I thought that some day I could take things to their limit and tell her an outrageous lie, and wait for her to guess the truth.

Paul Goodlands called in, and was asked to stay to supper, and did, and I found myself having a ridiculous conversation with him about handmade shoes, when neither of us had ever had a pair made for us; but we talked about them with great confidence all the same, and I think he enjoyed it, but not for the reasons I enjoyed it. And that was the evening I first began to think there was something between him and Norah, but then I imagined it was to do with him only trusting people from his own peer group, which Norah was, I suppose. And I think there was an element of her revenging herself on me for my friendship with Dougie by attempting to make the same sort of friend of Paul.

After he had gone, in the early hours, she said, 'He is such a sweetie.'

'Is he?' I said. 'I can't stand the man.'

She said, 'Don't say that. You had a really nice time. You know you did. Don't pretend you didn't enjoy it.'

I grunted.

166

She said, 'Well he's better company than your friend Dougie. He doesn't sit around all night looking like Eeyore.'

'Piglet, perhaps,' I said.

And she laughed. I had made her laugh at Paul Goodlands, and so I knew he couldn't mean that much to her. And it was strange to share a bed again, and not to be able to brush your teeth because of knickers soaking in the sink. She wore a vest in bed, and I said, 'Why are you wearing that?' And she said that she was cold, and I said, 'Take it off. I won't be able to sleep if you wear it.' And she took it off because I had flattered her. And it was bizarre to make love, and I don't know why. My three days of bachelorhood had made a deep impression on me.

And in the morning, before I was properly awake, she said, 'Were you pleased to see me?'

And I said, 'What do you think?'

She said, 'Did you mean that, what you said yesterday?'

And I said, 'No. That is my life. You have to look at things coldly sometimes, but you can't just throw your life away.'

And I think I believed what I was saying, and if we had gone to Herefordshire that day I might still be there now. But no, that isn't true. That is taking no account of my father.

But before things got worse there was a lull, and that in a way was the last week of our marriage. It was a time when there was terrible weather and I couldn't go walking, and Norah wrapped herself around me as the slates went crashing off the roof at night. And on Norah's birthday Jean came down from Shore Cottage with a cake and the children and there was a birthday tea. Norah loved it because she has always loved ceremonies of any kind. And there was a dinner party sometime that week in the big house, when someone complimented Paul Goodlands on the wine, and he said, 'Yes, it's very good, isn't it? It's a shame to throw it around.' And we both noticed after that that he only half-filled the other glasses, and kept the bottle by his own, and we laughed about it afterwards.

I saw Dougie twice or three times, but at the back of my mind I still thought that he was insane, and I hadn't yet reconciled myself to it. Later, the question of his sanity seemed trivial, and now I can see that he was probably the sanest man I had ever met. Or perhaps I mean that he was the most honest, and that he was the only man of whom I could say that I had seen both sides of his sanity. But still, even when I thought the worst of him I was fond of him.

And do we allow the word love to be spoken?

It was during that week that for the first time, when Norah said, 'Do you love me?' as she had said almost every day of our marriage, instead of saying yes as I always had, I said, 'There is no such thing as love. It doesn't exist.'

BOOK FOUR

I have had enough of this. I can't go on in the first person. From now on you will have to think of me again as a ghost, disconnected from Adam Parnell. It will seem strange to you at first but you will soon get used to it. I can see now that although I was Adam Parnell once I have become something else, in an altogether different dimension. And I might have to tell things that Adam Parnell could not have known. And wouldn't it be strange if I wrote about my own death in the first person singular? It has been done, but by a South American, and you are allowed these things in hot climates where reality is blurred by the forces of nature. But this is a Scottish winter, and the air is soft and cold, and heavy with truth.

In the third week of January news came to Joshua's cottage that Adam Parnell's Aunt Bridget had died. You could not say that her death was unexpected, but as it had been expected the past forty years, it was something of a surprise. Neither did she die as a result of one of her many illnesses, but was carried off in an epidemic of flu that was raging across Ireland at the time. She had been declining steadily since the time she had been a mentor to Adam. When she had become too infirm to bend or kneel in her garden, when Adam was fifteen, he had arranged fishboxes on trellises around her stableyard, and moved her collection of rare Alpines into them so that she could carry on gardening at waist-level. Over the years there had been a correspondence between them, which was mostly lists of Latin names incomprehensible to anyone else. He brought treasures back to her from England and planted them in her fishboxes. She collected and saved seed for him, and posted them to him in old pill bottles, and as her writing was not very different from her chemist's it was sometimes hard to tell which was the name of the plant and which the name of the drug. Adam, naturally, would go to her funeral.

He asked Norah to come with him, and she said yes at first but changed her mind the next day. She wouldn't say why but he knew that it was because her period was late and she was full of hopes. She wasn't prepared to risk air travel, which she felt might bring her on and destroy the possibility of a child. She knew that if she admitted her reasons he would blind her with science and bully her into going just to prove her wrong. She preferred to trust her instincts and stay at home. She said, 'No, I would only be in the way. And Irish funerals are so exhausting.'

'We aren't complete barbarians, you know,' he said. But he didn't argue any further. Once it was decided that Norah would stay in Scotland he began to look forward to burying his Aunt Bridget in quietness.

It was his father who collected him at the airport and drove him down. He had a through-ticket to Waterford, but the connection wasn't until the afternoon and his father was in Dublin that morning anyway. His father was already in a dark suit and black tie. Adam's weeds were in a bag which he threw in the boot. 'There's no point in looking like the Mafia until the last minute,' he said.

Well, that was fine. They talked quite freely until Naas, where Adam asked his father to pull up by a cash machine, and while he was waiting for his money he noticed a small boy of eight or nine standing close to him and holding out an empty plastic tub. The boy was neither clean nor well dressed, but he wasn't a tinker either. He didn't have the mark of that race or the professional attitude to begging that tinkers have. He was embarrassed to be standing there with his tub, but all the same he managed to say that he was hungry, and could he have the price of a bag of chips.

Adam put his hand in his pocket and produced what change he had, and at the same moment a wad of ten-pound notes rose out of the machine at him. He put the change in the boy's tub and stuffed the tenners in his pocket.

But instead of thanking him, which I am not saying he should have, at the sight of the tenners the boy put on a pathetic face and voice, and said that he had no shoes to go to school in, and indeed when Adam looked down there were filthy bare toes coming out of the ends of a pair of old trainers. But instead of compassion Adam felt a surge of anger, and trying to control it he said to the boy in as reasonable-sounding a voice as he could manage, 'Sorry, I have no more change,' and tried to get back to the car as quickly as he could before he exploded. But the boy followed him, contorting his face into a more pathetic expression with every step, and he stood close to the car as they drove away, unwilling to lose his initial advantage and a soft touch.

Adam was saying, 'I hate that. I hate it.' He was shaking a little with some kind of rage, and at the same time trying to work out why he was so angry. At first he thought he was angry at the boy, because he tried to justify his own meanness by saying that the boy would only have spent the money on glue or computer games. But then he couldn't see why a boy with nothing else in his life shouldn't be able to amuse himself with glue and computer games, and there was also the possibility that he would do as he had said and buy new shoes, although this would have been a professional disadvantage to him. And then he thought he was angry at society; at a town as prosperous as Naas, that would allow a boy like that to be begging in the streets, a boy who looked as though he might have some intelligence about him; and then the anger was for the boy again, who didn't have the dignity to starve quietly; until at last he knew that he was angry with himself for being too mean and middle class to give his money to the boy, all of it, if necessary, or to take the time to talk to the boy and find out why he was in the state he was in. And all the time when these things were going through his head his father was talking to him, but he wasn't listening, only saying yes and no automatically in response to tones in his father's voice, as he had learned to do years ago in his father's presence.

But he was calm well before Kilcullen, and talking properly to his father, even though the conversation had been out of his control for so long that he was somewhat surprised by the content once he came back to it.

Christian Parnell was saying that he was about to go and live in London. To find a job and start again. Adam said, 'As what? Do you have somewhere to stay?'

'I'll find somewhere.'

Adam said, 'It won't work.'

'Why won't it work?'

Adam said, 'Because you have been a big fish in a small pond for too long. No one will know you there.'

'Maybe that's why I'm going.'

Adam said, 'It won't work. All of your life people have been picking up the pieces for you. You won't survive for five minutes before you start drinking again. And that's all very well here where people make allowances and know you. You won't like being a drunk on Victoria Station.'

His father said, 'It won't come to that. I know it won't.'

'Well, the best of luck to you.'

They were both quiet for a moment while they overtook a couple of lorries, and a hard rainstorm came towards them, and then Adam said, 'What were you like when you were younger? Before you drank; before you met my mother?'

'I don't know. Why are you asking that?'

Adam said, 'I wondered. I always thought there had to be some good in you for my mother to have married you. And I wondered how much you changed, and what changed you.'

'I don't know. I suppose things were very easy for me. I was supposed to have been sickly when I was a child, and I was never sent to school like the rest of them, and I could have whatever I wanted.'

'You were a spoiled brat.'

'I don't think so.' His father lit a cigarette while holding the steering-wheel between his knees. Adam remembered that in his childhood he had always seen this as a feat of heroism; when they were all jumping up and down in the back screaming at their father to pass all the other cars; and their father would tell them to hold tight, and do handbrake-turns at speed and they would scream with delight: a hundred and eighty degrees. His father said, 'It wasn't to do with being spoiled. It was more to do with life being too easy for me. In a way I was determined that that should never happen to any of you. In a way I drank because I thought that you would all be better people if you had a hard childhood. And you are.'

'Hang on,' Adam said. 'I'm not buying that for one minute. You're not telling me that you were propping up the bar for our sakes when you would much rather have been the loving father?'

Christian Parnell shrugged his shoulders and accelerated towards another lorry.

Adam said, 'And what about James? When did you last see James? The last time I saw James he was shooting up in a squat in Brixton,

174

and it took me twenty minutes of knocking to get into the place because his girlfriend thought I was a cop.'

It was plain that Christian wasn't going to answer that, and there was silence until they got near home, when Christian said, 'Do none of you have happy memories of your childhood? It can't have been all miserable. Can't you remember the times when we were all laughing?'

Adam said, 'Not when you were there. There are no happy memories with you in them.'

And Christian said, 'I don't understand it. I thought we were happy most of the time.'

James surprised everyone by turning up at the funeral, with a smart new car, and wearing a suit. He evaded questions about what he was doing, and muttered something about a job with a merchant bank. It was Rosy who hissed in Adam's ear that James had got into dealing in a big way.

Adam said, 'I honestly thought he'd be dead by now.'

Rosy said, 'That's a myth. If that stuff killed people so easily there'd be no money in it. Junkies live for ever, like alcoholics. That's the worst thing about them.'

James avoided his father, and refused to speak to him. Christian, not wanting a scene, didn't force himself, but there was a great deal of tension. They put Bridget's coffin into the ground, and Adam glanced around at his weeping relations and wondered why he was so unmoved. He had loved his Aunt Bridget as much as he had loved anyone, and he had loved her more than some of the people who were mourning her now. It wasn't until they went back to her house afterwards, and he went out to the stableyard to look over her fishbox garden, that emotion overtook him. He had to find an outbuilding far from the house for privacy while his ribs jerked and heaved and he bit on his wrist to silence himself.

Rosy found him, and she said nothing, but leaned back against a pig trough and lit a cigarette, blowing the smoke about her until he turned to face her.

'God,' he said. 'I didn't know it was in me.'

She said nothing, but only smiled at him, and searching for something to talk about, he said, 'Is he drinking again or what? You wouldn't believe the bullshit I had in the car down.'

175

Rosy said, 'Well, he had a bit of a lapse last week. But he's supposed to be fine again.'

Adam said, 'He isn't making sense.'

'He's always like that,' Rosy said. 'Come on and we'll keep an eye on him.'

Adam watched his father closely, and as far as anyone could tell he was drinking lemonade, but he kept making excuses to disappear, and showed an uncharacteristic interest in being left alone with the washing-up. When the gathering broke up he offered to drive Adam back to the airport for the evening flight, and even though Adam could have gone as easily from Waterford, his father said no, he would take him to Dublin.

This time they went by the coast road, because Christian had to see a man in Arklow, which involved driving around a housing estate for half an hour, before being told by a put-upon-looking woman that her husband wasn't at home. Adam thought of his mother, and of them spending their lives hiding from people because her husband wasn't home. He said to his father, 'I hear you had a bit of a lapse.'

'I had a couple of half-ones last week. That's all.'

'And today?'

'Today?' his father said, as if he could have no idea.

'Oh come off it. You were drinking today. Everyone could see you were. I can see it now. Look at you. You get slightly obnoxious when you drink, and your eyes start to bulge out like a parrot's.'

His father said, 'Bullshit. I'm the same as I always am.'

'No,' Adam said. 'You're the same as you will always be.'

It is true that when Adam made his next remark he had murder running in his blood. He would have liked to end his father's life. Perhaps the murder was only symbolic; it was only a way of putting his father out of his life for good, but he said, 'Do you remember I asked you if you had ever thought about suicide?'

'Yes.'

'So how would you do it?' Adam was excited by what he was saying. The words were giving him a sense of freedom, and power. He thought about Dougie Millar, and realised that Dougie Millar was the key to all of this, because the thing he had envied most about Dougie was his dead father.

Christian said, 'I'd get on a ferry. And throw myself off half-way across. With any luck they'd never find the body. People would just think I had gone away.'

Adam pictured it as his father spoke, and when the body had hit the water in the darkness he breathed a sigh of relief, and said, 'So what's stopping you? Why don't you do it?'

Christian said, 'I suppose I'm not brave enough.'

Adam said, 'It's all hopeless, so.' He was talking now in a sort of post-narcotic euphoria, divorced from his words but convinced that he was making sense, like someone who has taken cocaine. 'I can't see any future for you otherwise. You are only going to get older, not better. And what then? I'm not going to be combing the drop-out hostels of London to look for you. And I don't want to have you incontinent and living with me. Thomas would probably look after you. But that isn't fair. It is only because he is a soft touch. Because he sees himself as the family's guardian angel. Making allowances for you, the best I can think is that you are someone who is incapable of dealing with life. It seems obvious that you should take your chances in the next one.'

He thought, as he was saying it, that it was sound advice, kindly meant. And he knew at the back of his mind that his father was not the sort of person who committed suicide; that he was a procrastinator and that he didn't have the courage. And because he had just killed his father symbolically, he was beginning to feel kindly towards him; the way you can feel kindly towards the dead, the harmless dead.

They had stopped at traffic lights in Stillorgan, and Adam, who had been staring straight ahead out of the window, looked over at his father, whose tears seemed to be making no difference to his driving, and Adam said, 'Fuck this. Why do I always have this effect on people?'

Nothing more was said until the airport, when Adam felt his father's hand grip his across the handbrake, and his father said, 'I did my best. I promise you.'

Adam said, 'Well, that's all right then.'

Once he had reached Glasgow he thought that he would give himself a late supper at Rogano's before going out to the Highlands. He thought that he would have been all right if his father hadn't grabbed his hand at the last moment, and he found himself carrying his hand oddly, as if it had been changed by contact with his father's.

There was a wino begging in Prince's Square, and Adam heard

himself say that he was sorry but he had no change, and he walked on ten paces, and then turned back again and put everything he had into the wino's hands. Irish money, English money, Scottish money, the lot. And he ate a large supper, and was surprised, because the knot that had been in his stomach for months was gone. Only that afternoon, at the funeral, he had had difficulty swallowing a ham sandwich. But still, he couldn't help thinking that it would have been perfect if his father hadn't grabbed his hand.

Once he was back at Inverclachan, he slid into bed beside Norah without turning the lights on, and she complained that his skin was cold so he kissed her neck and made love to her until the rhythm of it drove everything from his brain.

Dougie said to him, 'You have changed.'

'How?'

'You are more yourself.'

'Is that better or worse?'

Dougie said, 'It must be better for you. But I don't know if I can deal with it.'

Adam said, 'Do you know what the worst thing was? It was when he had Thomas's child on his knees, and he was playing with him and kissing him as anyone would kiss a child, and talking to him in that stupid voice that people use with children, and I was burning with rage because there must have been a time when he did that to me, but I can't remember it. He couldn't sustain any affection until I was old enough to remember. I should have killed him off when I was three, and not waited until now.'

Dougie said, 'What can I say?'

And Adam said, 'You can say what you feel. Don't leave it until it is too late.'

'Too late for who?'

And Adam said, 'There is only yourself to consider.'

Norah was happy with the change in him. He seemed to her more like the man she loved. She woke before him the morning he came back, and she watched him, thinking how familiar he was to her. She thought that she would try again.

Paul had been down to talk to her the day before. His reason was that Lucinda had left him, which was not an unusual event, but his account of his troubles was so moving that Norah began to cry for him, and he had put his arms around her to comfort her, and then he had kissed her, and led her to the bedroom. She found it strange, to be seduced by someone who had been a friend for so many years. It was not like a seduction at all, because she knew him so well. There was something innocent about it; there was no excitement or curiosity. It left her cold.

It was when they were both bare-chested, and he was moving his hands on her back, and putting kisses on her forehead, that she said, 'No.'

'What?' he said.

She said, 'This is a stupid thing to do. I'm sorry.' And because she didn't want to talk to him about it, she broke away from him and picked her jumper off the bed, and went to wait in the kitchen.

At about the same time as Paul was seducing Norah, after he had dropped Adam at the airport, Christian was boarding the ferry at Rosslare. He hadn't checked the times of the boats properly and the one for Wales was gone. The ferry for France was about to leave and he took that instead, thinking that any would do. The sea was rough and they chained his car down so that it wouldn't roll around. He almost told them not to bother, but he remembered that it wasn't only his car they were considering.

The boat seemed to be deserted, because most people were in their cabins being sick. There were only a few hardened lorry drivers in the restaurant. He had several drinks at the bar, and then there was an announcement for the film that was about to be shown, and he went to the cinema. He was the only one in the audience. The projectionist was a college boy who had taken the job to pay his way. Christian fell into conversation with him, and they chatted through the film, which was about American policemen who wear leather clothes and kill a lot of people.

After the film, when he had drunk some more, Christian went out on to the deck and watched the big swells and the spray from the boat. But the sea seemed too vast and cold and he knew that he would never do it this way. So he went to the duty-free instead and bought himself a bottle of whisky and took it to his cabin. It was a relief to be able to drink whisky again after weeks of drinking vodka so that no one would smell it on his breath. He didn't sleep that night, but smoked and drank and stared at the porthole waiting for the light to come through it in the morning.

He hadn't realised that France was so far away, and the next day he watched two more films. One was a comedy and the other dragged on a bit about a very pretty girl who was frightened of something or other. He missed a lot of the plot because he spent so much time talking to the projectionist, who said that he was taking business studies, but seemed unsure of what it involved or what he was going to do with his life afterwards. But he was likeable, and amusing, and easy to pass the time with.

Le Havre was as strange a place as Christian Parnell had ever been to. He had never been to France before, or anywhere else for that matter. You can't count England as travel. He had forgotten to change his money on the boat, so he couldn't stop for the night, but he had a full tank of petrol, so he decided to drive straight to Paris, seeing that that was what most of the roadsigns suggested. He had to avoid the toll roads because he had nothing to pay them with. But there was no hurry.

He gave up trying to drive in Paris and abandoned his car, double-parked in the Rue St Jacques. He thought he would like to see Notre-Dame. He had heard of a Canadian tourist who had attempted suicide by jumping from one of the towers of the cathedral. She had landed on another tourist who was killed by the impact, but she herself had survived. Notre-Dame was only a black hulk of stone in the dark, and he left it behind him and walked along the right bank of the river, beneath the bridges where the cigarette ends of the male prostitutes glowed, and once he was near the river he knew that this would have to be it. It was a river he'd been looking for all along. The sea was too big.

He wondered if he wouldn't have preferred to jump in the River Barrow at home. The Barrow was noted for its success in drowning people. It was cursed to take three a year. But it was too late to go back now, and besides, his mother had always said that you shouldn't shit on your own doorstep. After a lifetime of ignoring her advice, he was prepared to take it just this once.

He went up on that wooden footbridge that crosses from the Musée D'Orsay to the Tuileries and walked to the middle of it. He knew that there were patrols on the river on the lookout for people like him, and he knew that the Paris police took a dim view of suicides. It was said that when they fished people out of the river they arrested them first, before giving them any medical treatment. He knew that if he hung around on the middle of the bridge someone might guess his intention. It was still dark and wet enough for him to be invisible once he had jumped. There would only be the splash.

It wasn't much of a splash, and his last thought was the realisation that he hadn't been seasick on the ferry. He had never known that he was a good sailor. He thought that this was a fine time to find out, and less than a second later he hit the water, and he was too preoccupied with the process of drowning to wonder any more about seasickness.

The day that the news of the suicide came through Adam and Norah had gone out for a walk. They had been preparing for their return to Herefordshire. They met the postman as they left the house, and then they walked on slowly, opening their mail. They were about fifty yards downwind of the house when Norah said that she could hear the phone ringing. Adam sprinted back to answer it and Norah walked on.

When he caught up with her again she was about half a mile along the shore, even though she had been picking up oyster shells and taking her time. He walked beside her saying nothing for a while and then began to pick up shells himself, but small shells, the colour of apricots. Norah said, 'You were a long time,' and Adam said nothing. Then as calmly as she could she said, 'So who was on the phone?'

Adam looked at her in a hard way, as if he was trying to hold the features of his face steady; if he answered her abruptly it was because he had to keep control of his voice. 'Thomas.'

Norah moved her mouth, but didn't say anything. Disasters had already formed in her mind.

Adam said, 'My father is dead.'

She turned to him with her mouth open, and something that was like terror in her expression. 'What?' she said.

He remembered his father breaking the news of his grandmother's death to his mother. He had come home late and walked through the room where they were all sitting, without greeting anyone, and when he got to the door at the other side he turned to his wife and said, 'Your mother is very ill,' and she, who was in a bad temper already because there was some reason or other why he should have been home early, exploded at him, and said, 'What am I supposed to do about it? I am stuck here. What is the point of telling me something like that?' And Christian Parnell, hiding his body behind the open door so that they could only see his head, looked wounded, as though someone had

183

punished him for a kindness, and said, 'I was trying to break it to you gently. Your mother is dead.' Before now, the memory of that incident had helped Adam to despise his father, but this time he could only see a man who was without the ability to live in this world.

He said to Norah, 'They found his body in the Seine. I never knew he was a romantic.'

She said, 'It must have been an accident.'

Adam felt that he had to choose between smiling and crying, and because it was Norah he was with, he smiled at her, and said, 'No, it wasn't. Only a man who is going to commit suicide leaves his car in the middle of the street without locking it. In a strange city. And it was me who persuaded the fucker to do it.'

The word 'fucker' brought Norah's tears on.

He said, 'You are right. There should be more respect for the dead. And besides, it is the first decent thing the man has done since I've known him. He should get some credit for that.'

Norah dropped the oyster shells she had been carrying, and they made a thin clatter as they fell, but Adam put his handful of orange and yellow shells in his pocket, and they walked on in silence, across to the other end of Canada, and Adam told himself that it was only Norah's presence that prevented him from weeping.

She woke him up that night because she said that he was shouting in his sleep. She tried to get him to say what he had been dreaming about, but he said that he couldn't remember. Then neither of them could get back to sleep, and they lay in the shadows, on their backs, not touching.

She put her hand into his, and said, 'This probably isn't the time to tell you, but my period is three weeks late.'

He didn't respond for several minutes, and then he said, 'So we both got our wishes.'

He was still awake in the morning, and Norah was asleep. He wondered for some while what was the best thing to do. He wanted to be alone. The most tempting option was to feign sleep when she woke up and have the morning to himself in bed. His other option was to leave the house quietly and go for a walk, but that had disadvantages. In the first place he wanted a bath before he got dressed, in the second he didn't know what he would have to face when he got back. He couldn't face jeopardising Norah's good temper.

Norah took the initiative herself without waking. She turned in her sleep and put her leg across him. He watched her sleeping face and felt the pressure of her leg and the warmth of her, and it is not that he began to make love to her, but in a situation like that you are already making love. When you have lived with someone that number of years and made love almost every night of them, you come to think of their body as an extension of your own, and so lust is not a hunger, but an automatic reaction.

Afterwards, when she had her arms around his neck and she was smiling at him, she said, 'I love you terribly.'

And he said, 'I agree with the adverb.'

He said, 'Will you do me a favour? Will you go on to Herefordshire alone? I want to be on my own for a day or two. I'll follow you.'

'All right,' she said. 'If you want.' But she didn't look as though she liked the idea. He pushed himself out of the bed and he went to run a bath. The water on Inverclachan came out of the tap a dark peaty brown. It was supposed to be good for the skin. He sat with the water up to his waist and wondered what colour it would be if blood was added to it. He wasn't thinking of killing himself just at that moment, but because the razor he used was one of those plastic self-contained ones, he was irritated by not having the option of opening a vein if he should decide to do it. He made a resolution to go into Achacloaigh and buy a safety razor, just in case he might need it.

He hadn't been to Achacloaigh for a long time. Mr Cheviot waved to him from the window of the butcher's in a friendly way, and he managed to wave back. When he had bought the razor, he went to the tobacconist's and bought a packet of cigarettes.

He was coughing and spluttering over his first cigarette, and Norah said, 'What are you doing?'

'I just wanted to see what was in it,' he said.

She said, 'I don't like the idea of leaving you alone if you are going to be killing yourself with those.'

He went away to find Dougie to be taught how to inhale, and Dougie said, 'You don't want to start on that.'

'It's all right,' he said. 'I'm not addictive.'

It took four cigarettes before he could keep smoke in his lungs without coughing. He said to Dougie, 'Have you heard the theory that there is no rest for suicides? That there is no peace afterwards

185

if you take your own life? So what can you do? I only want a bit of peace.'

Dougie said, 'Don't do it.'

Adam said, 'Why not?'

'Because I can't go through that again. I've wasted my whole life getting over one suicide. There isn't the time for another.'

Adam said, 'I can't cry for him. I have to do something.'

Dougie's mind was miles away, and his eyes were darkening, and he said, 'Some people don't even get the option.'

Adam said, 'Kerry?' And he walked round to the back of the other man and put his hands on his shoulders, and said, 'You needn't worry. I've thought about it but I can't. You know that business about the umbilical cord? And when I was two some other children hanged me in a game. I was cut down in time, but I had a weal around my neck for years. I think the indications are that I will die by strangulation. And you can't strangle yourself.'

Dougie looked up to contradict him, and Adam said, 'I'm sorry. I forgot about your dad. But I don't think I could do that. He must have been a braver man than I.'

That night, it had already been arranged for them to go to supper at the big house, because it was supposed to have been their last night at Inverclachan. Norah said they could cancel it if he wanted, but he said no, it was still her last night, and they should mark it somehow. And when Paul passed his joint Adam's way, Adam took it and inhaled as deeply as he could, and by the end of the evening he was past thinking, and it seemed to him that that was the state of mind he was looking for.

But Norah smoked too, despite her condition, and the dope had a different effect on her. Once they were back in their own house, they broached a bottle of whisky, so that they became drunk as well as stoned, and she began to scream at him and hit him in the face and thump him across the shoulders. He sat still as though nothing was happening to him, smiling at her from time to time, until she gave up through exhaustion. She tried to leave him in the middle of the night, but he hid the car keys, because, no matter what else, and what state of mind he was in, he couldn't let her go and kill herself on the roads.

In the morning she was full of remorse, and she said, 'I can't leave you this way. We shouldn't be parting under these conditions. There is no hope for us if I go away while you are hating me.'

But he put his arms around her and told her that he didn't hate her, and it would all be fine, not hopeless at all. He said, 'It was only the dope. You shouldn't be surprised if you take mind-bending substances and find that your mind is bent.' She put her lips to his and crushed them so that he could feel the line of her teeth, and he pressed back, but he didn't open his mouth.

After she had gone he opened the doors and the windows, and he bathed, scrubbing himself as though he wanted to remove his whole skin, even though it was tender in places where she had bruised him.